WHAT REMAINS

ALSO BY
NICHOLAS DELBANCO

Fiction

Old Scores
In the Name of Mercy
The Writers' Trade, & Other Stories
About My Table, & Other Stories
Stillness
Sherbrookes
Possession
Small Rain
Fathering
In the Middle Distance
News
Consider Sappho Burning
Grasse 3/23/66
The Martlet's Tale

Nonfiction

The Lost Suitcase: Reflections on the Literary Life
Running in Place: Scenes from the South of France
The Beaux Arts Trio: A Portrait
Group Portrait: Conrad, Crane, Ford, James, & Wells

Books Edited and Introduced

The Writing Life: The Hopwood Lectures, Fifth Series
Talking Horse: Bernard Malamud on Life and Work (w. A. Cheuse)
Speaking of Writing: Selected Hopwood Lectures
Writers and Their Craft: Short Stories & Essays on the Narrative
(w. L. Goldstein)
Stillness and Shadows (two novels by John Gardner)

WHAT REMAINS

NICHOLAS DELBANCO

WARNER BOOKS

A Time Warner Company

The Prologue, Chapter II and Chapter III have appeared, respectively
and in somewhat different form, in *Salt Hill*, *Salmagundi* and
Michigan Quarterly Review.

Warner Books, Inc., 1271 Avenue of the Americas, New York, NY 10020

Visit our Web site at www.twbookmark.com

Ⓦ A Time Warner Company

Printed in the United States of America

First Printing: November 2000

10 9 8 7 6 5 4 3 2 1

Library of Congress Cataloging-in-Publication Data
Delbanco, Nicholas
    What remains / by Nicholas Delbanco.
        p. cm.
    ISBN 0-446-52416-6
    1. Immigrants—Fiction. 2. German American families—Fiction. 3. Jewish
families—Fiction. 4. Jews—New York (State)—New York—Fiction. 5. New
York (N.Y.)—Fiction. I. Title.

PS3554.E442 W47 2000
813'.54—dc21

00-039895

For my father, Kurt Delbanco, in his ninety-second year

WHAT REMAINS

What thou lovest well remains,

                              the rest is dross

Ezra Pound

Prologue

London, 1984

Uncle Gustave drives me to the house where I was born. It is November, overcast and damp. He has remained in Hampstead, in the northwest of London, and I go there as often as possible; each time I travel from America to see him might be, I fear, the last. He will prove me—for many years—wrong. Well past eighty in the year I make this visit, he wakes up every morning without pain; "Madame La Fata," as Gustave likes to call her, has been kind.

But Madame Fate is growing inattentive and half-blind. If her name were Lady Luck, she would blow on another man's dice. By the time of my next trip he will have lost his license, having crashed cars once too often and fetching up too often in the local hospital. They treat him respectfully there, but forewarned is forearmed, says the nurse. Other people are at risk, she says, and when they take away his license it is for sideswiping a taxi and breaking a passenger's arm.

Gustave is a catastrophic driver: squint-sighted, shrunk into the right front seat, his white head barely visible above the dashboard, peering out. He advances wreathed in pipe smoke, gesticulating, blinking, elsewhere-focused and discoursing on statistics or what he calls the impoverished nature and essential vacuity of modern art. "It is," he says, "a desert; it means nothing to me, nothing, it is only an example of the Emperor's new clothes." A sentimentalist, he rails against all sentiment in others—but when I say I'd like to see the house I'd been a child in he says, "All right, why not, let's just have a look."

Aunt Steffi is more sensible, going everywhere by taxi or bus or on foot. "I'll call a car," she suggests, and he says, "Nonsense, we'll take mine." She gives him his umbrella and he leaves it by the door. From the front hall she waves goodbye, repeating, "Be careful, won't you? Do be careful, both of you, and come back in time for tea."

I offer to drive; he ignores me. When I was young he used to own solid upright vehicles with names such as Humber and Rover, but this is a little blue Austin with dents everywhere like warning signs emblazoned on the hood and sides and boot. In Uncle Gustave's increasing old age his automobiles have grown battered also, and it takes minutes to negotiate the doors. Then we start our journey: the business of keys, the grinding starter motor and the terrifying lurch of gears, the wide circles while he banks and turns, the narrowly missed trees and gates, the streams of traffic dammed and pedestrians fleeing like startled fish . . .

The hills of Hampstead are steep. He has no parking brake. We careen into curbstones and veer around lorries while I tell myself, as always, I'll never drive with him again and I'll hide the keys. "In my opinion," he says, "the human animal is the only animal that thinks itself a thoughtful one or that believes in belief. It is yet another piece of evidence"—he taps his pipe; ash, burning, drops—"that God, should He exist, and I of course do not believe it possible or have any faith in Him, is a humorist." The windshield wipers slap and squeal; there is no rain. "But we are provincial," he declares. "We admire what we understand, and what we understand is best understood in turn as a projection of the self . . ."

The pond at the crest of Hampstead High Street is surrounded by a roundabout. I had played there when a child, sailing boats across it busily and hunting frogs and fish. But there is much more traffic now, and I've been dreading our approach; there are horns and perturbation in the circle when we enter, the squealing of tires and screeching of brakes. Gustave shifts up, not down, and wedged between a pair of buses we advance. My uncle is remembering how, during the worst of the Second World War, when the English feared invasion, they took down important road signs and turned others in the wrong direction and were therefore certain that the German army, should it arrive in England, would be lost.

They had a point, Gustave says. It is impossible to find your way in this peculiar country, impossible to drive in a straight line even if the signs themselves are each correct. And this, he declares—spewing ash from his extinguished pipe and warming to the topic—is typically

English: a circle, an arrangement where you must defer and take turns getting on and off, a perpetual politeness such as one encounters in a queue. This willingness to go nowhere at all while staring straight ahead is, he says, a national obsession—the way these people stand so patiently on line. Or consider the arrangement for seating in the tube, those armrests that ensure you cannot touch your neighbor's arm, the little barricades erected for the sake of privacy and in such contrast to the democratic benches of America or the bodily proximity so natural to France.

"It is astonishing how seldom you see bicycles in London today, how very different it is in China, for example, or the Netherlands. In Amsterdam . . ." he says, and sneezes and, signaling left, turns right.

At length we reach the street where I was raised, Holne Chase, and find and park in front of Number 3. On this weekday afternoon there's nobody at home. I ring the bell nevertheless: an electrical two-tone chime. The house is much less grand than I remember: brick, imitation Georgian, a squat gentility across a patch of lawn. The great arching entrance drive seems just a little turnaround, and the mulberry tree not tall. While Gustave lights his pipe again I walk to the living room windows but see nothing through the drapes. Then I walk into the garden at the rear. The coop where we kept chickens has been transformed to a potting shed; the north-facing roof has moss on the slates, and I try to remember but cannot which one of the windows would be where I'd slept and which one was my parents' room next door.

So I close my eyes and *see* it: that memory palace, the past.

A coal chute appears at my feet, and a pile of coal I clambered to the top of, pelting my older brother; I was the King of the Castle, and he the dirty rascal. Next we'd change places and he'd throw the coal. A gooseberry bush with its plump fruit festoons the garden wall. Behind that curtain is a piano and behind that one a desk. The garage our father reinforced for use as a bomb shelter still has our cots in it, perhaps, and an old jar of marmalade and tins of powdered cocoa with which to weather the Blitz. For some time I wander around the locked house, full of nostalgia and what I can only call Proustian remembrance: *this* is the corner where *that* had happened, *here* is the window I rubbed at to peer through the chill wintry fog.

The fog itself is actual; we drive back to Lyndhurst Road. Our return is uneventful and the traffic sparse. Gustave repeats his theory that, of any period since the tenth century, our own is the most bankrupt in artistic terms; the visual arts—his field of expertise, for he had been a connoisseur of Old Masters and a prominent art dealer—are today defunct.

I have heard this discourse on provincialism before. I know his theories on religion, physiognomy and travel, his opinions as to clothing or what he prefers to call "costume," his preference in hats. A droplet appears at the end of his nose; he wipes it with his sleeve. He speaks about the life-force of an artist waning, waning, so that only very few and only the very greatest—Titian, Monet—continue to advance their work past seventy or eighty; when I ask him how he would rank Picasso he snorts and shuts the engine off and slams against the curb.

Over tea I tell my aunt that Number 3 Holne Chase is just as I remembered it, the perfect container of childhood. She looks up, adjusting her glasses, and says, "What?"

I repeat myself.

My absentminded uncle absently agrees.

Aunt Steffi is less vague, however: "Silly, you were born at Number 6!"

So all that Proustian recall was false, a misremembered past. My madeleine was chocolate cake, my gooseberry bush belonged to a neighbor; where *we* lived was three doors down. And though it seems funny and just a touch sad that history should prove so subject to revision, I've come to feel grateful for inexactness: the gift, as it were, of invention.

Book
One

I

Karl: 1964

To TRAVEL IN AN AIRPLANE is to see the world as Leonardo never saw it, or Gainsborough or Rubens or Velázquez. To look down upon the earth from sky is something quite remarkable, and it makes him feel fortunate, always, as though he has gained a perspective his predecessors lacked. Karl does not mean by this, of course, that Leonardo and the rest are his predecessors in terms of artistic achievement or the size of their respective gifts, but nevertheless he does have an advantage: no single one of the Old Masters looked down upon the earth. Tiepolo attempted to imagine it; Veronese too and Ruisdael and Hobbema and Tintoretto and the rest, but what they really saw were only the clouds' undersides, their unremarkable bottoms, and he can see the land and water from a goodly, *godly,* height.

It makes a person think. Globality, *globicity,* it gives a person pause. He knows these words are not yet current and that he has coined them, but in a hundred years or less the world will have no boundaries, no borders and no passports or customs declaration forms or guards. He is admittedly an optimist but it is realistic to be hopeful in an airplane when one looks upon the land or shining sea. His brother Gustave likes to say that such an opinion is nonsense, but the planet will seem seamless, with only the equator and the poles. Kandinsky and Cézanne, Karl thinks, would have changed their way of painting had they flown across the ocean and looked down. Woodrow Wilson comprehended this, although he himself did not travel by plane, and Trygve Lie and Dag Hammarskjöld understood it later, with the United Nations. The world contains no boundaries that matter when you watch the earth from outer space, and the wars that so preoccupy us and the border disputes that require attention look pointless from above . . .

He is not in an airplane, however. He stands at the top of his house. In Larchmont in Westchester County, New York, the first thing he did after purchase was add a third floor—a fourth floor, if you count the finished basement—underneath the eaves. Here they have built a bathroom and additional guest bedroom and a wall of windows with, most importantly, a studio; here he can keep his work-in-progress on the easel and be as messy as he chooses and leave out his brushes and paints.

His wife hates the smell of turpentine; she says she fainted, when eleven, because the painter Liebermann whom her parents hired for her portrait used turpentine-soaked rags; she had had the first of her migraines and could not endure the stench. Linseed oil is less objectionable, Julia admits, but it is also offensive, and sometimes—

between the smell of kippered herrings in the kitchen and the smell of turpentine—she claims she will go mad.

Yet the studio is Karl's domain. He has relinquished kippers but draws the line at oil paint, and they have reached an understanding that here he may do what he wishes and make the mess he needs. Because painting is not mannerly; it is not good behavior, and sometimes he believes that— were it not for good behavior—he might have been an artist, truly, and not what's called a Sunday painter or gifted amateur. On weekends and on holidays and, sometimes, in the very early morning or at night he goes upstairs and feels wholly at home in his house. In the kingdom of his attic he luxuriates in color, the wash and bursting rush of it, the shapes he himself has called into being in honor and rapt emulation of the world beyond. Beyond the window he can see the wide expanse of his own lawn, the trees that make a little park, the village in the middle distance and, in the far distance, the line of the Long Island Sound. This day it is a deep blue-green, a combination of green earth and ultramarine, and the sky above is cobalt blue and the moon still visible above the horizon: there, *there.*

~~~~~

"Do you see that?" he can remember asking.

"Yes," said Benjamin. This was when they painted together, when the boy was young.

"But see it. I mean, really *see* it."

"That's what Granny asks me."

"She asked me too. In Hamburg she was known to be—well, artistic."

"Peculiar," Julia said. "That's what he really means."

"No. Unconventional. It's not the same."

"Peculiar," she repeated.

"Just put your thumb in front of you, and measure between your knuckle and your fingernail the relative height of the tree . . ."

"I'll leave you two alone," she said. "I have work to do in the kitchen."

When Benjamin was four or five he used to like to paint, and they would take their easels and go out to the garden in Hampstead or, later, in America, to the waterfront in Manor Park and make pictures side by side. It had given Karl much pleasure, and the boy had a certain facility, a sense of line and shape. But every young child finds enjoyment in drawing and very few, as they grow older, retain it, and soon enough Ben's interest flagged; he turned to books instead. All three of their sons are bookish, of course—this is Julia's influence—but he had had some hopes that Ben might continue to paint. And this was not to be. Fading, *schade,* a great shame, since he himself has never lost his love of drawing or the visible world and up here in his studio he surrenders to it gladly; the work of import-export and the bristle business is nobody's business here.

Karl turns from the window and back to the mirror: he looks at his face in it, hard. Today he will finish the face. His project this morning is a self-portrait, not a still-life or landscape but, as his first teacher in Germany said, the landscape of a face. Four feet tall and two feet wide, it is canvas he stretched weeks ago, with his visage in the bottom right-hand corner of the composition, and a window and bookshelf above, *The Artist in His Studio*, and with a jar of brushes on a table at the left. He has done self-portraits often, since he sits for himself without complaint—unlike his wife who cannot bear the smell or his children who fidget or his friends who, at a certain point, consult their watches and say, "Sorry, I have an appointment, I simply must leave."

"Just a minute, just a minute . . ."

"I'm sorry, the car is waiting . . ."

"*Augenblick* . . ."

Then they disappear down the stairs.

Yesterday's brushwork has dried overnight. He switches off the fan. Like any other portrait painter Karl has made a study of his own facial structure and understands the distance, say, between his ears and the bridge of his nose and the distance from his eyebrows to his hairline and his upper lip to chin; he has examined himself with sufficient attention to take no present notice of the length of bone or the planes of the cheek and how they intersect. In Rembrandt's great series of self-portraits, for example, it is not the likeness that comes into question but rather the mood and the light. What varies is the artist's age, and what he is wearing and how he displays it, but not the architecture of the face as such. After forty, said Abraham Lincoln, I hold a man's face against him. The face itself, *Das Ding an Sich*, the proportion of the eyebrows and the nostrils, the relative width of the lips . . .

The arrangement belongs to Matisse. In the upper left-hand quadrant of the composition Karl has positioned a

bottle of whiskey—he might change the J&B label, however; it looks too specific and he might decide to erase it
today—and an apple and a fruit knife and a loaf of bread.
It had been a conscious homage, a tip of the painter's cap,
although of course Matisse did not drink scotch but wine
and his own compositions were lighter, flatter, more in-
vested in design.

He is fifty-five years old. His eyes are brown. What
hair he retains is gray-black. The nose is prominent, broad-
nostriled, and he paints himself wearing large brown horn-
rimmed glasses and with the weekend's stubble on his
cheeks because this early Sunday morning he has not both-
ered to shave. To bathe before painting is wrong, or anyhow a waste of time; to bathe afterwards is welcome, and
then a person shaves.

The face is good. The open white shirt and the neck
and mottling of the cheeks and forehead—from yellow
ochre to burnt sienna—is adequate, at least. What troubles Karl is not the face, its arrangement and proportion
and knowledgeable innocence, but rather where it sits on
the canvas and how it belongs to the larger idea, the change
in the nature of space after Sputnik: what relation we bear
to the world.

~~~~~~

This is his third country, and it will be the last. He left
Germany because of Hitler and England for Julia's sake.
Had it not been for the Nazis he would have remained in
Hamburg, and had it not been for Julia's conviction that
their sons would thrive in the New World he might still

16

be working in Leadenhall Street and very prosperous there. His elder brother prospers; the gallery in Cork Street has done very well indeed, and Gustave does not seem to mind that to the English his accent is strange and his clothing peculiar. I am what I am, Gustave says. Yes, Julia says, and what you are is fortunate to work in a profession where what counts is expertise and not what they call the school tie. But for my boys I want no prejudice, I want a land of opportunity where they are not a bloody foreigner and have equal opportunities; my boys will go to Harvard, she declared once the family had settled down, and in the course of time first Jacob and then Benjamin did as their mother had wished.

No doubt their third son, William, will also attend Harvard College. No doubt in the matter of where they should live his wife was as usual correct. There is, Karl knows, the landscape you are given and the landscape that you choose; often it can be the same, and then you do not need to move, but the landscape of the heart is difficult to find. He means by this that the person who lives in the mountains but was intended to sojourn by the seashore will be discontented, and vice versa, and never quite understand why. Likewise the person who was born in Rome might perhaps belong in Oslo or the person who calls Paris home should instead live in Peking. The trick of human relations, as well as human happiness, is to know—how should one put it?—the heart's geography. This does not mean, *natürlich*, that the river in and of itself is better than the lake or the lake than the ocean or the ocean than a desert, but in any case you must decide which is your own chosen landscape and try to make it your own.

17

When young he had traveled to Venice and found the place his ancestors once lived in—a great stone pile in Dossoduro, on the Grand Canal. The Palazzo Bernardo, John Ruskin wrote, is an imposing edifice, and Karl's ancestors had occupied it in the sixteenth century; this offended the senators of the Republic of Venice, however, since they themselves could not afford so grand or so spacious a home.

And in part because of this they ordered every Jew to move to one surrounded place and proclaimed a ghetto where the ironworkers worked. Let us live in Murano, Karl's ancestors begged, we will purchase the whole island, but the Doge said no. Let us be surrounded by water, not iron, his ancestors petitioned, and the Doge repeated his refusal and thereby in some measure spawned that history of horrors: the *ghetto vecchio*, a separation of the Jews amounting to quarantine. In 1630 his family left Italy; in 1670 his ancestors were driven from Vienna and traveled on to Hamburg and resided there in comfort until Hitler threw them out. It isn't a question of whether but when: death and displacement will come.

Wind rattles the north-facing windows, here at the top of the house. When you look down upon the earth from twenty thousand feet it is impossible to see inside the desks of office buildings, or the inside of men's minds, and everything that's venal or corrupt gets leached away. At the far wall of the garden, the maples bend and wave. No doubt an Albert Einstein or an Albert Schweitzer could manage a global philosophy and understand the ways that good and evil intersect. No doubt Mahatma Gandhi or Jesus or Gautama Buddha could view with equanimity the behavior of the German people during the Third Reich; it would be wonderful, Karl thinks, to see the world in terms so high and aloof and abstract. From the perspective of an airplane, it does not matter much. From the perspective of a satellite, it scarcely matters at all. But such an attitude is, for him, too difficult to manage and such perspective too hard to attain; the inside of men's minds on *Kristallnacht*, he neither forgives nor forgets.

And it could happen here. On a daily basis it is wise to be prepared. When John F. Kennedy was shot, and then Lee Harvey Oswald on TV, he had been fearful of madness, *Wahnsinn*, a national catastrophe, and they would have to leave. All over America Karl was afraid there would be looting and rioting and windows smashed by men with guns. The man who shot Lee Harvey Oswald was not in the hallway by accident; Jack Ruby was a man they let into prison as part of their plan, and soon enough, he had been certain, there would be mass arrests. Once you have been a refugee you never forget it could happen again.

And so he said to Julia, "Where should we keep the packed bags?"

"What bags? What are you saying?"

"I want to be ready."

"For what?" she asked.

"In case we have to leave . . ."

"We won't," she said. "I promise you. Bobby Kennedy will find it if there's anything to find."

"But if more than one person murdered his brother . . ."

"No."

"No?"

"We do nothing till it's proven that there has been a conspiracy, and President Johnson would tell us. He would be forced to tell us, because Bobby would certainly know. And will bring the killers to justice, of that you can be sure . . ."

The north light is sufficient now; he turns off the overhead lamp. She had been right about that also, Karl reminds himself, tying his smock; in the months since the assassination his fears have been allayed. On that fatal day, November 23rd, and in the days just afterwards he had believed that madness would be general and the murder of President Kennedy was part of a general plan. In his office they were saying that the martyred President had been shot with the prior knowledge and perhaps with the assistance of the FBI. There were news reports and articles and interviews that blamed the Mafia and Cuban exiles from the Bay of Pigs and the CIA.

But even in the worst of it—and the worst is over now, the Warren Commission is doing its work—he never quite believed that they would have to flee. In America live honorable men like Walter Cronkite and Joseph P. Welch and Chief Justice Warren, and they keep the nation honest and they will keep it safe. These people are too decent for such a thing as *Kristallnacht* or the abominations of the Gestapo and the Wehrmacht and SS. So even in the period of that terrible McCarthy, or during the war in Korea, even in the time of the Cuban blockade and then the missile crisis, America is hopeful; you can tell it walking down the street or by the names in taxicabs, the way the drivers of the taxis come here from all over the world . . .

In Hamburg his father had been privileged to serve as civil magistrate and to decide, in business matters, what penalties to levy and which taxes to impose. He had been one of two such judges and it was an important post, but during the Third Reich, *natürlich*, all of this would change. One day his father was informed—by the weasel Sollen- rad—that the locks on the doors had been altered and his position would have to be relinquished for "medical rea- sons," and he should resign. Within the week his father had been diagnosed for cancer, and within the year he died, so there had been great irony in the suggestion he save face by resigning for reasons of health. Too, Uncle Ernst took poison when they took away his job; he had been very eminent, *Herr* Director of the hospital, and when they decreed that no Jews could administer a hospital he wrote a letter to his colleagues deploring what had hap- pened and went to his own private office and swallowed arsenic. When they discovered him next morning the news- papers made quite a fuss; they wondered if there might have been irregularities of bookkeeping or perhaps some sort of scandal or a romantic intrigue; they did not print his letter or announce the actual reason that the *Herr* Di- rector died. Because the actual reason was a government decree, of course, and Uncle Ernst was too proud to ac- cept it and would not resign. Then second cousin Eliza- beth jumped out of the window in Bremen when they came to collect her, so that had been two suicides in a single generation, not to mention those who were in fact sent off to Buchenwald and Bergen-Belsen and Auschwitz and

21

Dachau. The great Mephisto, Hitler, danced a dance upon their graves.

~~~

Across the sound an airplane rises glintingly from the direction of La Guardia; another plane descends.

It is nine o'clock.

Karl rolls up his shirtsleeves and takes off his watch and adds paint to the palette. He considers the tubes of alizarene carmine and cadmium red, then rejects them: too garish, too bright. He first visited America when he was twenty-two. In 1931, when he had finished his apprenticeship in his father's firm, his father said, Why not a *Wanderjahr*, why not enjoy yourself a little bit before you settle down? We will manage without you a little bit longer, and soon you must be serious but not just yet, not now. I will send you to America and you can have a wander-year and sleep as late and be just as lazy as ever you wish.

And this was what he did for months; he had never been so lazy in his life. In the school years at *Gymnasium* and then, later, in the office when the wandering was finished and during and after the war, *natürlich,* and now making a living in import-export he has always kept a schedule, and the schedule is full of appointments, a supplier or a customer to see. This is what it means, he knows, to be successful, the head of a family and with dependents—the office staff, the household staff—with clothes and cars to buy and a balance sheet to balance, the taxes and school bills and mortgage to pay. These are the trappings of responsibility and therefore a person must work.

But in 1931 it had been *Gute Reise,* a good journey and a period of peace. He lived alone in Greenwich Village, on the corner of Waverly Place, with no telephone or wireless and, of course, no television, since such things were not available; there had been nothing but his cot and chair and chest of drawers and, down the hall, a bathroom. The cleaning woman appeared once a week and rearranged the dishes or the small pile of his shirts. From his second-story window he could observe the traffic: cars and carts and what had seemed an endless promenade of men who worked in offices, going in and out of buildings and bustling on the crosswalks and past the changing lights. There had been a promenade also of men who went nowhere but stood in the sunshine or sat on the front steps of buildings and folded and unfolded newspapers and smoked cigarettes. For those were the Depression years, and many citizens were idle, and it had seemed acceptable to have no occupation and no one to report to; his allowance was more than sufficient and his needs were few.

He made friends with a student from Prague. This morning Karl remembers the fellow's face precisely, the sharp hooked nose and beetling brow, the way his front teeth overlapped, and the blue woolen cardigan his friend had worn all winter, and its missing buttons, and the way he rolled the sleeves. The two of them drank coffee together, and tea, and cider, engaging in impassioned conversations about the way to ease the burden of the masses and thereby improve mankind's lot.

They went together to the Metropolitan Museum and admired the collection, the Raphael and Rembrandts and the astonishing sarcophagi and the Grecian urns. At the museum with his copybook Karl spent hours copying the back of a well-muscled soldier or the arch of Cupid's bow. On the steps one afternoon he met a girl from Düsseldorf who said she would meet him in Washington Square, but although he waited in the snow at the appointed time and place the girl did not appear. She had had a dancer's upright posture and splay-footed stance; her hair was tied back with a bow. He cannot recall the girl's name, of course, if he even ever knew it; they would never meet again and it was of no consequence. But what troubles him this morning is he has forgotten his comrade's name also—Pavel, Janos, Franz?—and now thirty-three years later it is peculiar, is it not, that he should have so clear a memory of a dark blue woolen cardigan but fail to remember a name . . .

"*Verweile doch, du bist so schön.*" This is Goethe's phrase. This was the agreement Faust arrived at with the devil: he never would or could be so enchanted by a single moment that he wished it would not change. As long as Faust remained both restless and unsatisfied, he would be permitted to live; no moment would appear so beautiful he would regret its passing, and as long as he had no regrets he could continue on. When I declare, *Verweile doch*, the philosopher had boasted, then you may take my soul from me and it will rest in peace.

For Mephistopheles, of course, the bargain is an easy one and sooner or later he'll win. He offers riches, beauty, fame, and the mortal man accepts them turn by turn but is not beguiled. His devil's compact lasts quite a long time; for most of the poem Johannes Faust submits to but is not seduced by temptation. What he *is* seduced by in the end is work, good works, the reclamation of the land from sea and how it brings prosperity and safety to the people of the region; this brings him satisfaction and he says to the passenger moment, please stay, and is on the instant condemned. "Remain awhile, you are so lovely," Faust cries and therefore dies.

But nothing is ever so simple, in Goethe or in life. The line that damns him is the line that saves him equally; the desire to help others is the cause of his salvation. When Julia was in her second and difficult labor, when Benjamin was born during an air raid, their neighbor Mrs. Plimsoll crossed the street, carrying a pot of jam, and she had seemed an emissary from the charitable world. The jam was homemade; the Plimsolls had a very good plum tree in the corner garden, and it yielded quantities of plums. "I have heard your wife shouting," she said. "This will make her feel better, poor thing."

Such was the decency of England, the kind concern of wartime, and although Karl has lived in Larchmont now for as many years as, earlier, in Hampstead, he does not regard his neighbors the same way. Americans are friendly people; they call you by your first name, always, and say, "Hi," and wave and keep their lawns mowed and their hedge lines trim but do not bring you jam.

He turns to the floor-length mirror behind him—a composition grows more clear when examined in the mirror—and, studying the canvas, shuts his good right eye. The cheekbone has been smudged, he sees, and so he takes a palette knife and incises the line of the cheek. Next he pours an additional measure of turpentine and linseed oil into their tin cups, then caps the bottles carefully and returns them to their shelf. In 1931 he had been his own master; he could stay in bed all afternoon or not go to bed until six o'clock in the morning and nobody complained. He took long solitary walks, circling *endlich* back to Waverly Place or choosing to continue and be lost, a little, but never in a way that mattered, since he had made no promises or appointments and therefore had none to break. He did take painting lessons in a studio on Bleecker Street and afterwards sketched men in threadbare jackets, waiting on the corner and selling apples to the passersby; he drew children at a fire hydrant and, in the windows of the shops, the hanging sausages and the plucked scrawny fowl. His teacher said, Yes, yes, you have a real facility for line. You are not advanced with color and you should pay attention to color, but line is something else again; line you understand.

At night Karl listened to *Die Dreigroschenoper* or that peculiar form of American expression, jazz, and when summer arrived he grew restless and continuing his *Wanderjahr* took a Greyhound bus across the country—visiting the Mississippi and Grand Canyon and Yellowstone Park. He improved his English and his understanding of the problems of perspective: how to establish the vanishing point and where the light must fall. In villages and cities and in landscapes with a ruined hut or abandoned copper mine he drew and drew and drew. But he had been an innocent, a nearly total innocent, and when a woman in the Greyhound bus station in Phoenix said, We could get off here together and have a good time, he said, *Entschuldigen Sie*, I do wish to see the Grand Canyon. She looked at him, astonished, and collected her handbag and left.

Verweile doch, du bist so schön, is something he said often then, for this is a form of indulgence an adult rarely knows. Karl traveled alone; he ate and drank by himself, sparingly, in restaurants; he went where no one he knew would have been able to find him, admiring the buffalo and the alien corn. His father and he exchanged letters, and every week he sent Elsa his mother a postcard with a picture of the sights. He sent her the Statue of Liberty, the Brooklyn Bridge and Old Faithful and, from Colorado, Pikes Peak. In New Mexico he bought a turquoise bracelet and a matching ring and necklace for her, from a man with a face like an Indian mask; he also bought bright weavings and intricately fashioned ornamental bowls. And now that he himself has sons he wishes to be generous, as openhanded as his own dear father was, enabling them to make their way untrammeled in the world . . .

~～⌐

Karl adds a spot of Naples yellow on the too-white shirt. Then he daubs yellow ochre lightly where the white shirt meets the neck. He had primed the canvas with sienna and raw umber and left it that way to begin with, but it makes the portrait somber, too serious this morning, and he wants to improve the mood of the picture and bring it up from too-great pessimism into the optimistic range of colors: yellow, a single spot of orange above his horn-rimmed glasses and, elsewhere, a bright green. He puts an orange highlight on the bottle in the background and feathers out the label, J&B, then changes the slope on the shoulders of the bottle also, so that now it looks like wine.

27

Next it is time to decide on the wall. Attentively, meticulously, he selects a two-inch brush. From time to time and for the sake of variety he likes to draw or use watercolors or pastel, but his chosen medium is oil. He orders his supplies from Grumbacher and Winsor & Newton, and because he is in the bristle business, he can recognize the quality of the kolinsky or the badger hair and how well or loosely they bind it; he uses only the very best brushes and paints. Again he considers the cadmium red and, once again, rejects it, but vermilion yes, vermilion possibly, why not? The world itself, he tells himself, is coming out of darkness and why should his self-portrait not reflect just such enlightenment, the end of a dark age? Globality is what one sees, globicity is the wave of the future, he's sure.

Julia calls up the stairs. *"Karlchen,"* she calls. "Have you had breakfast?"

"No."

"Well, do you want anything?"

"Nein, danke."

"Not even coffee?"

"I drank some orange juice," he lies.

"All right, then. Come down for coffee when you want it. And croissants, we have croissants."

"Later, thank you. I'm all right."

"I'll leave you alone, then," she says. "But when Billy wakes up we'll have brunch."

There are books in the bookshelf behind him: *Buddenbrooks, Der Mann ohne Eigenschaften,* two auction-house catalogues of African art and an illustrated volume on the lost wax method and one on Donatello and the notebook of Paul Klee. He pulls out and leafs through Paul Klee. For he has lost the gift of concentration; he imagines their son Jacob where he works now in a hospital or Benjamin living in London or Billy eating a croissant, and everything else—the Greyhound bus, *Kristallnacht,* Waverly Place in a snowstorm—all of it flies from his head. He should not have allowed himself to think about his father; it has made him feel sorry, and sorrow is nothing from which one can paint. Desire, Karl reminds himself, is something else again, it is altogether different and a source for painting, often, as in *Déjeuner sur l'Herbe.* Or the women of Courbet.

He had hoped to be an architect; his best friend in Hamburg became an architect and they might have studied together after finishing *Gymnasium*; it would have been a pleasure to build buildings, and he has an eye for design. In Manhattan he deplores the way the space in skyscrapers confines the men who work there, rather than releasing them into open air. The Lever Brothers Building and the Seagram's Building are, to this rule, exceptions; they have been designed with care and those who work inside them must be happy and productive, and every time he sees them Karl approves. In public or in private rooms he notices proportion, and how *der Goldene Schnitt* pertains, and how much more productive it would be to live in harmony. But his brother chose to study art, and their father expected a son in the firm, and he had had no choice. And now that he himself has sons from time to time he has wondered aloud if one or the other might enter the firm, but Julia said, "Over my dead body," and that was effectively that.

She has no respect for business, has taken it for granted, always, believing money grows on trees and it is beneath her to concern herself with how it has been earned. If he reproaches her for spending in a fashion that's extravagant—the piles of shrimp, the dozens of shoes, the quantity of orchids that she orders from her catalogues—she says, "The problem isn't that I spend too much but that you earn too little; we must have more money to spend. I thought many things about our marriage, I thought about it long and hard, but one of the things I never considered was that I couldn't buy shrimp." When she speaks this way it is pointless to argue, but if he dares to mention that their expenditures might be reduced she offers him her phrase about fate, *"Tu l'as voulu, Georges Dandin."*

This is supposed to mean, he knows, that Georges Dandin embraced his fate, that Dandin wished for something once and cannot complain when in the end he receives it. He, Karl, does not complain. At the bristle merchants' convention last spring, a meeting he attended by himself because Billy had a fever and Julia would not leave the house, at the Greenbriar Resort in the mountains a woman with too much to drink came up to him and asked if he would care to dance and after they performed a foxtrot said he was an excellent dancer. She said why don't we sit one out and have a drink together; he agreed. They had a pleasant chat and drink and then she suggested they go to her room and continue the entertainment upstairs. He told her no, he was happily married, and when he told this story to Michael Kasdan at breakfast next morning—not being specific, of course, not pointing to the lady in question at the corner table—Mike said, *"Sie sind überheiratet."*

But there is no such thing as overmarried, no pleasure

like the pleasure of this home to return to at night. The wife he proposed to in England, who said, "We might as well go through with it," has been his true companion since and he believes when optimistic that she too has no complaints. He has been a good provider; that much she will admit. There is nothing the family lacks. The rest is a matter of good luck or bad, a question of globality, and though Julia concerns herself with what will happen to their three boys on a daily, an *hourly* basis, he thinks about it less and less and thinks more and more about the flow of capital in outer space and the remarkable prospect of the United States of the World and how Tiepolo would render clouds if he looked down not up.

For the truth is Karl enjoys his office, and he likes the work. He likes it that his father's father went to Russia every year in order to buy fur and hides, and then his own dear father for two decades did the same. It is not a tradition exactly but a form of expectation: what his father and forefathers did is what he learned to do. He has done what was expected and will not complain.

The nature of the business has altered in this country, however, and synthetic fibers have increased their market share. Because of the embargo on supplies from mainland China, where the best bristles come from, he cannot make much profit as a bristle merchant; his London partners no longer require his office for their China trade. Therefore at the suggestion of his accountant he has branched out into paint sleeves and the import-export of artificial Christmas trees and wigs, and next year is preparing to import Italian bicycles; he does not mind that he must work in order to keep up this establishment—the gardener, the laundress and the maid from Switzerland who takes care of their youngest son and cooks. To be *überheiratet* is a pleasure; to be standing in a studio is fortunate; to have survived Mephisto has been his great good luck.

He hears music in the living room, but faintly, it is far beneath: Vivaldi, perhaps, or Telemann, a composition by Bach. The pattern of it—not the melody but rhythm—rises through the floor. What he is proud of are his wife and sons; what he enjoys is for five days a week to earn a living in Manhattan, and then on weekends and on holidays to climb up to his kingdom and complete a portrait of the landscape of a face. He is no good at hands, has never had success with them, and therefore keeps the image of his own two hands off the canvas—the right one below the brown plane of the table, the left at the end of the sleeve. What he wants is just to get it right, to render it *exactly*, so that years from now a man may say, standing in front of this portrait, yes, that is what it looked like, that's the way it was.

II

Benjamin: 1944

THE THING HE REMEMBERS to start with is light. It plays about his mother's face; it falls from her teeth and the whites of her eyes and the powder she pats on her cheek. The powder comes after the cream. The powder is both pink and white, and she pats it with a yellow puff and then he gets to hold it and the Yardley makes a cloud. In daytime when they are allowed the window pours in brightness; at night there are candles and lamps. At night they must close all the shutters and put the piece of cardboard up and also close the blinds. At night there are torches they hold to their chins, and then the chins are red. The light is everywhere, is everything, and even when he shuts his eyes the light is outside, waiting, and in the shelter when it's dark Dr. Lucas says, Only two bombs.

Dr. Lucas is a fat man with a belt that holds his trousers up and cuts him in the middle like a pillow wearing string. He wears spotted ties and a tie clip with a ruby and his

33

shoes are polished brilliantly inside his black galoshes; he sits down on the bench inside the door. First he crosses one leg on his knee and, puffing, bends forward and pulls; he lifts the rubber from the sole not toe and then he bends back the galoshes and, with a sucking sound, they show his shoes, and then he leans back and leans forward again and does the same thing with the other leg and hand. *Pfft, pfft,* go his shoes; then they squeak. There is Dr. Samson also, and Benjamin prefers him since he always has a peppermint, and his eyes are blue.

Dr. Samson comes from Hamburg, Dr. Lucas from Berlin. Dr. Samson plays chess with their mother, and coming in the house he takes off his coat and he hangs up his coat and they set out the pieces and play. Once, when he was studying a move, their mother said, *Entschuldigen Sie, Herr* Doctor, but I have a sick child upstairs. And he said, Don't interrupt me, he'll be fine. Then he moved the bishop to queen four and then she said checkmate. Oh, all right, Dr. Samson said, I'll find out how the boy is feeling. I'll just step for a minute upstairs. The thing he remembers to start with is jam, because when she was birthing him she cried so much and shouted so loudly their neighbor Mrs. Plimsoll came all the way across the street and knocked on the door and told their father, Here, perhaps she'd like some jam. It will make her feel better, poor thing.

Well, he can't remember that, of course, you can't remember being born, but he does like strawberry jam. And when he asks for more they tell him that story and pass the cold toast. And when he asks for more again they say it's rationed, no, you have to make it last. You greedy blighter, Jacob says, that spoonful was *my* spoonful; find-

ers keepers losers weepers is what he answers back. Their
father Karl likes marmalade and when he says here, have
a taste, here, why don't you try it, Ben says no.

Where they sleep is the garage. His mummy and daddy
and big brother Jacob and sometimes the maid and sometimes Peter or Colin or Paul and, when she visits, Granny,
sleep there all together every night; his bed is by the wall.
It's the safest place, his mother says, and it has animals all
over: a donkey on the ceiling that his father painted, and
an elephant and Rafi the giraffe. He painted it one morning, and then they all moved in. Ben's bed is next to Rafi,
whose stomach is a rock, and his neck goes up to the ceiling and then bends down again. The giraffe's neck is yellow and brown. His tongue is red and right next to the
bed and licks grass that is also a rock: A.R.P. Air Raid
Precaution, it says. When their father painted it he made
it a surprise; he said, We'll want some company and you
should have some animals here also to inhabit the garage.
When the war is over, Granny promises, we sleep upstairs
again. When will that be? he asks her, and she says, *Hoffentlich*, soon. Dr. Lucas says only two bombs.

Granny went to the grocer's on Tavistock Hill and said,
I need some oranges, my son's a fire warden and he's fighting in the war. Would that be for juice? said the grocer,
and she said, *Entschuldigung, was?* Would that be for juice?
he repeated, and she turned to Paul and whispered, Let's
get out of here right now. Why should we go, asked Paul,
before he gives us oranges, we've been waiting half an
hour on the queue? Because he is anti-Semitic, she said,
and from such a person I refuse to buy these oranges for
juice.

When Paul tells the story he laughs. It isn't funny, says their mother, if you hadn't gone along with her we would have had no fruit. You must learn to pronounce things, she says, so the grocer's clerk will pay attention and he'll know. There's a difference between juice and Jews and when Ben asks her what, she says a world of difference, a world. Then she peels him his half of the orange and divides it into sections and he sucks. The light is everywhere, is everything, and when he swallows brightness, sweetness, he can hear himself humming, he hums.

But the best is milk chocolate to suck. It comes from Switzerland, they tell him, it's very hard to find and keep and get with just a ration book and comes in squares. When the war is over, Mummy says, we'll go to Switzerland and eat all the chocolate we want. Lindt, Toblerone, as much as and whenever you want. Not possible, his brother says, will you watch that greedy blighter well he's always eating isn't he, he's got chocolate all over his face. And so when they lie in the shelter at night and there are bombs and searchlights he gets a piece of Cadbury's to suck. Because it's like a wafer for the *goyim*, Granny says, it's the child's version of salvation and the certainty of brightness and so she rocks and cradles him and says there there, little mister, *doch doch*.

~~~

But their father knew their mother long before there was a war. His parents met in Germany when they both lived in Germany; he came from Hamburg and she from Berlin and they met at a concert, he knows. It was chamber music at the house of the Cassirers, and Madame Cassirer introduced their father to their mother and said why don't you sit together for the music? but his father said I can't, I'm sorry, I'm not speaking to my uncle and my uncle's in the room. How very peculiar, his mother thought, and she says it was just this peculiarity that commended the young man to her attention, and when Ben asks her what she means by "peculiarity" and "attention," she explains. In a concert in a private house you sit where your hostess suggests. You don't change your seat if your uncle's nearby, you don't simply leave the salon. They were playing Schubert, the "Death and the Maiden" quartet. But she wasn't used to meeting gentlemen who didn't want to sit by her and so she went out to the garden after Schubert and he was standing there and this time was polite and so they talked.

She tells Ben what it looked like—apple blossoms, linden trees—and what it sounded like—four stringed instruments, the scraping chairs, the clinking of glasses and clatter of plates—and how Karl explained that his mother was having one of her quarrels with his uncle and therefore he was forbidden to remain in the same room. Granny was always having quarrels then, always making someone welcome or refusing them the door. But his father's uncle was the famous one, *Herr* Director of the hospital, and later on he killed himself because of Schicklgruber which is what Granny calls Hitler, and everyone forgave him and wished they had not quarreled and had been there to help.

"Did you like him?" asks the boy.

"Who?"

"Daddy's uncle."

"Not really. He was vain."

He looks at her. She's smiling. She kisses his forehead which he calls a forest; she kisses his forest then pulls at his ear.

"He simply assumed that you knew who he was. *I* didn't know," she says.

"Did you like Daddy?"

"Yes, of course."

"But right away?"

"He made such a spectacle," she says. "Of course I would like him for that."

Franz Schubert wrote symphonies also, and they whistle and sing the *Unfinished Symphony* to say they're just around the corner and are coming home. Their father whistles the opening notes and they answer with the next. *Babum, ba ba de dum,* he goes, and the children go *ba ba de baba de dum dum.* It's a code we have, he tells them, a secret way of knowing when you lose your family and need to find us again, it's a secret way of saying friend not foe. If ever you get lost, he says, just remember Franz Schubert; I'll know.

What got lost is Mummy's ring. She has a gold ring on her finger with the head of Minerva inside it who is, she says, a goddess from old Rome. It was a piece of money once, and you will get some money when you find it, she tells him; she tells Jacob too. It is probably outside. The ring stays on her finger, but the head of Minerva popped out of the gold, and because he is called Ben the looker he goes outside to look. You can see the place inside the ring the head of Minerva popped out. Will I get a shilling? Ben inquires; no, a sixpence, Jacob says, and Mummy says a pound. It's a ring of real value, she says, and not just sentimental value, do find it for me, darlings, won't you please? When you find it you'll get a reward.

So they both begin to look. It probably happened, she tells them, between the car and house and is therefore in the garden or the driveway or the lawn. He is known as Ben the looker because he found Granny's thimble and he found a four-leaf clover and a sixpence on the carpet and the place in the hot-water bottle where the hot water leaks. He will beat Jacob, no question, and they begin on the lawn.

He begins at the door and walks to the car and then he walks backwards and does it again. Minerva is brown and has only one eye and a nose that grows straight from her forest and Ben can remember the way that she looks but she's not in the grass or the gooseberry bush or anywhere under the tree.

He begins at the tree and walks to the car and then he walks backwards and does it again. The grass is wet and difficult and when you look closely there's pebbles that come from the driveway, which is where Jacob goes.

Ben starts at the car and walks to the bush where he kneels and then stands up again. They get yogurt and a cup of juice and keep on looking forever and when Mummy comes outside at last she says don't bother it's not that important, in a way that means except it is. I'll survive, she says, except your father gave it to me when we got engaged. But are you certain, Granny asks, you lost it here? and Mummy says yes certainly, where else? And then Jacob goes whoop whoop here it is, and he bends to the driveway and reaches through pebbles and picks up Mi-

nerva, whoop whoop. Oh darling, she says, oh that's wonderful, thank you enormously and thank you both so much.
But *he* is Ben the looker and Jacob's just a greedy blighter
with a pound. It's not fair it isn't fair, he says, and crybaby, his brother says, fair and square.

Well the principal thing is you found it and I'm very
grateful, Mummy says, and then she turns to him and says
well you should get ten shillings also for helping to look.
Crybaby, Jacob says again, but *I'm* the one who found it
and this must be my reward. Well the principal thing is
the ring in my hand and everyone should celebrate and
see how it fits in the gold. *Doch, doch,* Granny says, just
don't cry.

———

"What's that?"
"What's what?"
"That one." Granny points with her cane. Her real name
is Elsa, he knows.
"An oak tree."
"Correct."
They are on their nature walk. She is enormous and
walks where he runs. The wood of the cane is from Africa,
ebony, and the place you hold it is a silver snake with eyes.
She points.
"A beech tree, Granny."
"Which one's that?"
"Also an oak tree."
"Correct."

And because he has named three trees in a row he gets a jelly and sucks.

"What kind of flower is this one?"

"A tulip."

"*Ach ja, Tulipen.* And that one?"

He doesn't remember.

"You knew it the last time." She points with her cane.

He finishes the jelly.

"I told you what it's called before. *Gestern früh.*"

He can't remember. He could if he tried to. He can't.

"An iris," his grandmother says. "Like the iris in the eye, *verstehst du*? And that tree, what do we call it?"

"A monkey tree?"

"Correct, my little monkey."

"Can I have chocolate?" he asks.

Then it starts to rain too badly since the nature walk is finished and they eat a dish of yogurt in her room.

"*Morgen früh,*" she tells him. "Tomorrow on our nature walk when I show you the iris you'll know."

～⌒∽

So Teddy and he go to visit the place where he best likes to sit and they rock. Teddy sits on his lap near the gooseberry bush and Benjamin tells him a story and pushes his eyes; his eyes are brown marbles with black. Teddy's ears get pulled and twisted and he squeaks when he stands on his head. Jacob comes into the garden and says oh put that thing away why don't you, oh and help me here's a spade to dig. He is five and Ben is two years old and he says more than twice as old and so you have to listen and obey. Then what they say they cannot hear because the sky is roaring and the noise is enormous and louder and they look and see a plane, a brown plane just over the tree. Mummy runs out from the kitchen to look and she's shouting what they cannot hear and throws them down by the gooseberry bush and Teddy falls there too. Jacob's crying, Ben's not crying, and she says oh my darlings my babies it's the Luftwaffe isn't it yes. And later Paul says well it was bombing the East End but it just flew away over Hampstead and she says so near so near I saw the pilot's goggles and his yellow scarf.

But they must leave London instead. They will travel to the Isle of Wight where nobody bombs houses or drops bombs along the gardens and they can visit the sea. It is only for a little while and some of the children don't go with their mothers but Mummy and Granny do visit the sea; if they didn't go with Mummy they would have to go with children who travel by themselves. Colin and Peter are fighting the war and Colin they call Baron because he is brave and dangerous and Paul will go to Cambridge except he doesn't now. He came to them from Germany and is Mummy's second cousin which means cousin once removed and he plays excellent cricket and will teach Ben how.

The train up to the Isle of Wight has places for the family, and Jacob sits with Granny, which is why he makes a face and says there isn't room. I must make myself a place, she says, I must arrange my things. Jacob pulls his mouth wide with his fingers and squinches his eyes shut and sticks his tongue out twice. Ben says look *look*! and points at his brother and tells them but nobody sees. Their father took them to the station and will be there just as soon as possible and surely in a fortnight and he wishes them safe journey, *Gute Reise,* and stands waving when they leave. When he puts his nose against the glass it flattens and his father smiles. When Ben kisses the glass and then moves away his mouth is on it still. Lucky England is an island which means everywhere around it is the water and it's time, their mother says, that we should pay a visit to the water which protects us and makes us all safe. In the history of England no one beat it from the water except nine hundred years ago when William the Conquerer landed at Hastings, Mummy tells them; the Spanish tried and then the Germans tried and everybody failed. What about pirates? Jacob asks, and she says pirates never even dared. And sometimes pirates worked for England too just like Sir Francis Drake.

But what about planes? Jacob asks.

Those are new, says Mummy. Those are inventions of this century and the reason why we're going for vacation to the Isle of Wight.

But Julia, it isn't a vacation, Granny says, it's an evacuation. Let us call a spade a spade.

My my what a big puddle, Ben tells Mummy by the sea.

When will Daddy come? asks Jacob, and she tells him in a fortnight, perhaps sooner, soon enough.

Ben's eyes are brown and his hair is black and Mummy says he has her skin. He is, she says, the apple of her eye. What about Jacob? he asks her, and she says I have two eyes. When it rains and they go walking and he asks what about the rain? she says are you made out of sugar are you afraid you will melt? In the Isle of Wight they sleep in the same room again because this hotel is overflowing, Granny says. She wears only one color and everything matches; one day it's gray and tomorrow it's black. If she wears gray shoes, Granny says, then her skirt and her pullover and even her scarf and her gloves and hat must equally be gray. If she wears black, however, then the rest of her costume is black. It is her decision, she decided long ago, because that way the jewelry stands out by contrast and when he asks her what that means she say, Here, and points to her necklace and bracelets and ring. It is silver, always silver, only the vulgar use gold. That is my opinion anyhow, she says, and I have always had opinions and am never afraid to express them; well that much is true, Mummy says.

Mummy's mummy is called Omi and already in America where she and Opi have escaped and Daddy's mummy is Granny and a person with opinions; there are *Sinnlichkeit* and *Sittlichkeit,* she says. There's the life of the mind and the life of the body, and you are too young to understand but someday you will understand it, Granny tells him; everything can be found right here in Boethius. She carries the book of Boethius everywhere, a black book that fits in her pocket, *The Consolations of Philosophy,* and also cigarettes.

"Let's go swimming," Jacob says.

"We can't. We're not allowed."

"Why not?"

"Because."

"Because why?" he asks. "Give me one good reason."

"Bombs."

"It will be our nature walk," says Granny. "Today we will study the water."

So they get in their trunks and go down the stairs and the hotel has buckets and spades. There's a blue glass bubble in the hall, and inside sits a paper bush and on it six stuffed birds. There are carpets on the stairs he bumps down bumpingly, and the first time it didn't hurt and so he goes a second time and Mummy says enough. My my what a big puddle, he tells everyone, because they laugh, and when he does it every day they tell him that's enough. *Das ist genug,* Granny says. She is enormous and wears no bathing costume because in my day, she announces, we didn't learn to swim. Swimmabimma, Granny says. But every day they can go to the beach and make castles in the sand to keep Schicklgruber out, and if a wave knocks it about then they just build again. They build moats and a drawbridge and towers and thick leaning walls out of sand. When will Daddy come? asks Jacob, and Ben wants to know that also so he cries. Mummy rocks in the rocking chair, smoking, holding her cigarette holder, and says there there don't cry. He is doing business, he can't just arrive at the seashore, he is putting out fires at home. Do you want to take your chances back in London? Granny asks her, also rocking, also smoking on the balcony, and she answers yes.

So then they take the train again and Daddy meets them at the train and kisses his mother and wife. That's what they are, but the boys are his two little masters, my dears, and he shakes both their hands. And then there's so much luggage that they take a taxi home, and Ben gets to sit on the small folding seat and hold Teddy and his suitcase on his lap, and Jacob does the same. Not with Teddy, never Teddy, because *his* bear is called Pooh-Pooh and it stinks. The fog is bad, the driver says, pea soup this time of night. Turn left here, Daddy tells him, it's just the other side of Primrose Hill. But when they climb up Primrose Hill they can't see the street or the sign where they turn or the driveway and house, and Granny says *ach, furchtbar,* what a climate what a town. Well it's better than smoke, Mummy tells her, and at least there won't be any air raids, not this evening or tonight. Did you miss me? asks their father, and they tell him yes oh yes. Did you learn to swim? he asks them, and Jacob says smashingly, yes.

So then the driver says I can't go any further, guv, not in this fog it isn't possible I can't see the first thing. And then their father climbs out of the car and says just let me have your torch and follow on behind. And he walks out in front of the headlights and they follow very slowly in the taxi and Ben wants to walk beside him but Mummy says you two boys stay right here.

What he remembers to start with is darkness, the thick yellow fog at the window and, when they roll down the window, Granny coughing and Jacob complaining, of course, of course, and saying he wants to get out. *Nacht und Nebel,* Granny mutters, Night and fog. Careful, *Vorsicht,* says their mother and the driver says you're Germans, are you, why don't you go back where you come from, but he doesn't want to go back to the Isle of Wight. The thing he remembers is darkness, the dark, till their father steps up to the window and puts his face inside smilingly and says stop, thanks, this will do it, we're home.

III

1945

HOME IS NUMBER 6 Holne Chase, a brick house with leaded windows and a pebbled driveway circling past the entrance door and, inside the vestibule, a mask. Their father has nicknamed this object "Mephisto"; it comes from Java, its visage is fierce. He has hung it in the entryway, he informs the children, in order to scare off intruders — so every time a robber comes the robber will be terrified and just run away. The mottling of the face is green; its eyes are black and tongue sticks out and there are black horsehair whiskers thickly protuberant from the chin and wooden cheeks. It's a demon mask, Karl tells them, and Mephisto is our name for it and it will keep you safe.

There are many masks inside the house, principally from Africa, with a secondary grouping that includes New Guinea and the Marquesas Islands and Japan. Their grandmother started the collection back in Hamburg when nobody else understood it, she says, and everybody said such masks were a stupidity, a madness. Picasso understood, says Elsa, and Schmidt-Rottluff also, a little, but most people don't comprehend what they look at, they simply fail to see. When Benjamin touches a mask sheathed with skin he asks if it is human, and his father says not human, no, it's antelope, it comes from the Ekoi.

There are knives and a jade blade, says Jacob, for cutting off your neck. There are many neck-rests made of wood which are, their father tells them, a pillow down in Africa, but his brother whispers it's what you rest your neck on when they plan to cut it off.

"This one's from Dogon, can you say that?" his father asks, and Ben says, "Yes, Dogon."

"This one is Bambari."

"Bambari."

"And this one belongs to Baoulé, can you say that?"

"Baoulé."

"And this copper mask—they used metal very early— comes from a place called Benin."

There are, he learns, the Gold Coast and Congo and Ivory Coast and those shields on the wall are South Seas. There are monkey skulls with beaded beards and long-beaked birds and bobbins for weaving and ornate carved ebon-wood clubs. But what about the knives, he asks, but what about these feathered spears and then the curving horn? Dr. Samson tries to blow the horn and Jacob attempts to perform on it also, but neither of them manage. *Whoosh whoosh*, they go, *poot poot*. Ben fits his lips to the ivory rim, feeling cold wet bone beneath his teeth, and blows into it fruitlessly. What emerges is spittle, not sound.

His brother says, "There, silly-billy, I *told* you you couldn't, you see."

There are holes at the edge of the antelope mask and that's where you thread raffia, but raffia's a kind of straw not Rafi the giraffe. Then the tribespeople cover their bodies and dance; it must be, says his father, something wonderful—remarkable—to see. Closing both his eyes and stretching out his arms and spreading and shaking his fingers, Karl says, "When the mask-eyes are closed it's a dead person's mask; well, some of them are sleeping and live inside the spirit world and then you put it on over your head and antlers make you eight feet tall and then you dance all night."

Uncle Gustave pays a visit, and after lunch he puts Mahler on the gramophone and says, "Now watch me dance. Watch me dance until I drop," he promises, and pulls the antelope skin head over his own and lurches through the living room, his blue serge trousers and striped tie contrasting oddly with the fixed rictus of the beast that masks him. The children laugh. Their uncle, encouraged, flails his arms and imitates a tribesman, shouting, "*Whoo whoo whoo*," behind the wooden teeth embedded in the crescent of the mouth. "*Whoo whoo whoo*," he moans repeatedly, prancing to the music, lunging at his nephews where they quail. At length Gustave ceases—a little stutter step, his right foot raised, his elbow wedged up against the piano— and says, "Enough. *Genug.*"

But then he cannot take it off although he pulls and pulls. The Ekoi mask is double-faced, facing both directions equally, with carved striations on the cheek and a small pointed conical hat. Their uncle cries, "Help, help!"

his voice high-pitched and muffled, until finally Karl seizes the neck and together the men pull it off. The face beneath the mask is raw, flushed, peering, blinking. "Oh, I was just pretending, really," Uncle Gustave says.

"*Furchtbar,*" says his grandmother, when Ben asks about the neck-rests and what sort of pillow they make. "Imagine lying on the ground," she tells him, "with a wooden pillow for your head; imagine that the prince and king—no matter how important—still have to lie on the ground."

Then Paul comes in the door and picks up the rhinoceros tusk and, with a studied negligence, places the horn to his lips and blows through it loudly, piercingly, the sound a clarion. "Oh, listen," Ben says, "listen," and he sings, "*Poowha, poo-wha.*"

Paul says, "It's nothing, really," and then he produces a handkerchief and wipes off the rim of the horn. His father died in Germany and the families are, although distantly, related, and so he was sent to Great Britain, having taken a freighter from Nice. Soon he will embark on his studies in Cambridge, but now he is on holiday and stays with them all in Holne Chase. "His daddy died because of Schicklgruber who is," says Elsa, "the devil incarnate—but Winston Churchill will fix him, old Winnie soldiers through. So you mustn't be frightened," she says.

Paul teaches Ben to whistle, to purse his lips not smash them, and when he learns to whistle it is unalloyed delight and what his father calls a joyful noise. "Is that what soldiers do?" Ben asks. "Is that what Schubert did?" Because when his father whistles Schubert the boy can answer back, and he practices each morning by the chicken coop. Paul himself takes no pleasure in whistling, although Benjamin has heard him do it smashingly, and never wants to talk about what Schicklgruber did; he says that there are certain things it's better not to know.

"Can I ask him?" Ben inquires.

"No."

"Mummy, will *you* ask him, then?"

"We'll see."

When she tells her sons this it means yes.

"What did Schicklgruber do?" he persists. "Why did Paul's daddy die?"

"He killed himself," says Julia. "So they wouldn't kill him first . . ."

"And where's *his* mummy?" Jacob asks. "Where did she ever go?"

Their mother spreads her hands. She examines her red fingernails.

"*Dans la présence des enfants,*" Elsa says.

Their mother turns away.

⌁

Jacob attends the Annemount School, which is taught by Miss Jamaiker; it is just around the corner and then up the street. Next year when Ben turns four he'll get to go to Miss Jamaiker's, and Jacob will go to the King Alfred School, but meanwhile the two brothers take what their grandmother calls a constitutional each morning after breakfast and Ben and his mother fetch Jacob for lunch; they see a hedgehog in the hedge and Julia says, "Don't startle it, it's sleeping and it won't hurt you asleep."

Their father's partner Johnny Weiser does a parlor trick.

He invites the boy to step on his shoes and he moves forward and Ben steps back, holding Johnny by the belt, and they go dancing up and down. There is music on the gramophone or Johnny Weiser hums. He is fat, with two round chins and a solid protuberant stomach, but unlike the grim Dr. Lucas he is affable, good-humored. Arriving, he removes his coat and says, "Well, come here, Mister Blister, let's do a waltz, one two three."

"Oh, Johnny," Julia says, "will you look what he's done to your shoes!"

"It doesn't matter," Johnny says. "They shine right up again, and it's good for us to celebrate"—he pats his stomach happily—"the Battle of the Bulge."

So Benjamin holds Johnny Weiser's belt buckle, and they move together one step forward and one step back. When Mr. Sterner visits, however, he doesn't get to dance; Mr. Sterner runs the factory in Kentish Town and he is lean and severe. "Your father's business partners are like Jack and Mrs. Spratt," says Julia. "Because one of them will eat no fat, the other eats no lean."

The reason they can stay in England, the boys know, is Chunking two-three-quarter. One afternoon two policemen arrived while their father was taking a bath, but he said, "Just a minute, just a minute," and promised he would go with them to Golders Green. "I must just finish my bath," Karl said, "I will be with you shortly." The policemen had been patient; they stood beneath Mephisto, chatting, and their shoes were brightly polished and they shook their heads politely when Julia offered tea. Then she telephoned the solicitor Sir Robert Witt, and Sir Robert called the constable down at Golders Green and said this gentleman's important for the war. So the three men went off to the station and as soon as they arrived the constable said, says their father, "Yes, *sir.*"

"Because of the bristles," he explains, "and how the army uses them in order to clean guns. We have one hundred cases in the factory in Kentish Town, and Chunking two-three-quarter is the perfect thing for cleaning guns, since it comes from the neck of a pig. Just there above the backbone," Karl says, and shows the boy, and puts his finger on Ben's neck and says, "Well, let's see, Mister Blister, could we be using *your* hair for the barrel of a gun?"

Other Jews have been deported; they are being sent to India or Australia or to Canada, but this family remains in London because of the war effort and Chunking two-three-quarter. "Now isn't that remarkable," says Julia, "that we've been permitted to stay in Great Britain because of the neck of a pig."

"It's the way of the world," Elsa declares. "It's all here in Boethius," and she pats the worn black leather cover of her book. It's what they mean, she explains to the boys, by a "letter of credit" and "banker's draft," and therefore the solicitor Sir Robert Witt could telephone to Golders Green and say let this gentleman stay.

In the garage Rafi's tongue is a rock and it licks by the side of his bed. When they settle to sleep Karl returns to the house and says what a fine night it is. He says, "Outside tonight there are stars." And then he hums Brahms's lullaby and asks Ben, "Can you whistle for me, will you perform a tune?" And the boy is proud and gratified and purses his lips in order to whistle and says, "But Jacob

can't." And there's another song he knows and it goes like
this:

> *Deedle deedle dumpling, my son John*
> *Went to bed with his stockings on.*
> *One shoe off and one shoe on,*
> *Deedle deedle dumpling, my son John.*

Jacob has been taught to read and torments his younger
brother with what he learns in school. They look at the
pages of *Henry's Green Wagon*, and Jacob can read it aloud.
Ben looks at the pictures and follows along and recites
what he has memorized, but his brother can recognize the
letters and he says, "You don't, you can't. Which one is
this if you're such a good reader?" he asks.

Ben tells him, "E," and Jacob says, "Yes, all right, which
letter is this one?" and points.

The book finishes with Henry who has been playing by
himself and has green paint on his face and hands, because he found a can behind the greenhouse and painted
his wagon and then the puppy and the wall. On the final
page young green-cheeked Henry says, placatory, smiling
at the cook, "Oh, Bessie, I'm a little messy." She wipes her
hand on her apron and has been planning to scold him,
but he smiles his charming gap-toothed smile and says
Bessie, I'm a little messy, and when Ben repeats this aloud
to the adults the adults indulge him and laugh. Then Jacob
shuts the picture book and puts it on the shelf again, saying, "Blighter, go to sleep."

"My husband," Elsa says, "was a sunshine man. *Verstehst du?*"

The boy tells her yes.

"He was the perfect gentleman. My chevalier."

"What does that mean?" Ben inquires, and she says, "A chevalier is gentle and always has good manners near the ladies and wipes his mouth before he drinks and is polite. 'Thanks awfully,' he says. A chevalier will use a fork not fingers and he isn't cheeky and he doesn't ever shout. His name can be Lohengrin or Lancelot or Bayard, but my husband's name was Ludwig and you must grow up for my sake to be a chevalier."

He promises.

"My sunshine man never complained," she says.

"About?"

"The office or the family and everyone he had to help because he was head of the house. To be a Jew with money, my sunshine Ludwig used to say, is to have your table always full and relatives you barely know who ask you for a loan. When we gave our Sunday morning breakfast it was famous all over Hamburg," she says. "There was so much food and such good food they came from miles around."

His grandfather, Ben knows, had died before the war. "If he had not died," says Karl, "I myself would not be here." He says this not to Benjamin but to Dr. Samson, who has time for just one game. They are playing chess; they study everything about the board, they tell the boy, and look for position and traps. "You must always ask yourself," explains Dr. Samson, "what move your opponent makes next."

"When my father died," says Karl, "it was possible for me to leave but otherwise I could not have left, and we would not have managed."

"If I say check, what does he do? He moves his bishop *so*."

"And if I move my knight instead, he moves his bishop *so*."

"But he might have understood," says Dr. Samson, finally, and Karl says, "No, no. When I took him to the hospital he was too weak to raise his head, and there was a banner across the road that said, *Juden raus*. And he lifted his head only a little and said, 'What is that, what what?' And I told him, '*Gar nichts*, nothing, don't worry,' and so he never knew how bad it was before he died."

"I am sorry for your trouble, Karl," says Dr. Samson, "but if I move my rook like this it's a forced mate in three."

"It was a private hospital too, a place where Jews could come to die," his father says. "*Ja, wohlgetan*, congratulations, I resign."

Ben knows other twice-told tales, a repertoire describing where the family has come from and, by implication, where he himself will go. Their father's house in Hamburg was on the Inner Alster and its garden finished on the steps to a canal. "In Hamburg," says his father, "there are the Outer Alster and the Inner Alster, can you say that?"

Ben can: "*Aussenalster, Binnenalster*."

"Yes, it's a waterway in town. The way that London, for example, has the River Thames."

When his father was a child he had a rowboat in back of the garden, which gave out on the canal. And he would row to school, he says, that is, when the weather was fine.

Uncle Gustave too would row to school, and the brothers raced. But one day when he was eleven years old, according to the story, Karl climbed to the top of the house, and there was a statue leaning out, a lady with what you call a block-and-tackle for bringing up furniture and, for example, *zum Beispiel,* a piano to the music room on the second floor. And he took a piece of Granny's underclothing and tied it to the lady and no one else could get up there to bring it back and so it flapped and flapped. And everyone said *Wunderbar,* there is Madame in the wind. It was a joke, it was only a joke, it was a very funny joke, but Granny did not laugh. The upstairs maid was Trude, and finally she reached it down and brought it back inside. And so I was punished, says his father, smiling, and for weeks I could not row myself to school.

But her own house, says Julia, was bigger, with a fountain in the garden in Berlin. The rooms and all the furniture had been designed by Heinrich Tessenow, and Tessenow's assistant was Albert Speer. *Herr* Tessenow, their mother says, said this young man is very gifted but his character is bad; you must watch him closely while he's working in the house. And this was true, she says to Ben, *leider* Speer became the principal designer of the Third Reich and Hitler's architect. When she herself would go to school the chauffeur drove her to the corner, because she did not like to let the other children see she had a chauffeur. "I was always shy about it," Julia says. "In Hamburg are canals," she tells the boy, "but Berlin has proper avenues and streets. If you come from Berlin then you look down your nose at any other city, because it is provincial . . ."

"What is that?"

"Provincial means unimportant," she says, "provincial means you could not bear to live there all your life."

Then his grandmother goes sniff sniff, and his father goes *"Hummel Hummel, Mors Mors,"* which means you come from Hamburg and are proud of it. "It isn't bad to be born there," says Karl, "to be so to speak a native of the town."

"My chevalier," says Elsa, "you must learn about good manners, and one of the things about manners is you don't insult your host."

"Well, what about that time at the Cassirers'," Julia asks, "when your son refused to sit where he had been instructed for the concert by my side?"

"Well, that case was quite different, and Julia you know it was," says Granny. Then his father repeats, *"Hummel Hummel, Mors Mors,"* and his mother goes out of the room.

～✑

What he likes best about Holne Chase is the dining room, because in the cabinet there they keep mints. The cabinet is oak, and locked, and has fourteen shelves for silver with a place to put the knives and forks and serving spoons and ashtrays, and inside the custom-built shelves each piece of silver fits. There are soup spoons and demitasse spoons and what that signifies, Ben learns, is half a cup in French. There are dessert spoons and sauce spoons and every different kind of spoon has separate slots lined with green velvet for the silver to fit in. This is true for fish forks also, which are different than meat forks or salad forks, flatter, with a picture of a fish along the handle, and there are five kinds of knives. He distinguishes them by the handle and blade: *cake knives fish knives knives for salad knives for meat and knives for fruit.* His mother leaves the key inside the keyhole of the chest, saying, "We must trust each other, don't we, not to eat more than one mint."

She confides this to him smilingly. "You may smell them if you like, and you may look at them also but only eat one every day. And the silver paper on the chocolate is how best to keep it fresh."

"Keeps the doctor away," says Paul, and laughs, and then he says, "Well come on, Mister Blister, let's go into the garden and help me fetch the eggs."

On the cabinet sits a humidor—yellow oak to match the cabinet—and there they keep cigars. "First you cut them," says his father, "then you lick them, then you light them, then you smoke."

"Come on," says Paul, "I'm waiting, and I don't want to wait any longer for my scrambled eggs at lunch."

He is off to Cambridge now but when he visits he is hungry. "So hungry I could eat a horse," he says, and with one hand rubs wide circles on his stomach; with the other he pats his own head.

"Poor boy, poor boy," says Julia, "you will be welcome here as long as ever you wish."

On the wireless they listen to Prime Minister Churchill, whom the adults call "Old Winnie" and who will "soldier through." He lives in Downing Street and wears a bowler hat and smokes cigars continually and he will save us all, says Julia, together with his good friend Franklin Roosevelt. When Hitler turned to Russia and took his planes away from England, she says, then *endlich* I thought we could win it and decided *Der Führer* has made a mistake. She is smart about these things, their father says, she is a very intelligent woman, your mother, and when Hitler turned to Russia she said we might survive. Let's have a second child, she said, and then he smiles at Benjamin and, ruffling the child's hair, declares, That's the reason you are here. Mrs. Plimsoll from across the street could hear it and brought jam. It will make her feel better, poor thing.

The boy sits and listens, half-asleep, to the adults talking, taking comfort in proximity, their complicated memories and runic muttered utterance. He inhales the smell of lemon, of cigars and tea and chocolate and schnapps and furniture wax. On the wireless Old Winnie goes growl growl. Everybody pays attention and they stop what they are doing; don't fidget, his grandmother says. Pawn to bishop six, says Dr. Samson, attention Karl or I will take you *en passant*. He will never beat the English because right is on our side. He will never win, that devil, because President Franklin Roosevelt is helping with the war. But it didn't always seem that way, it was a near-run thing. We are hopeful now, we were not always hopeful, says his father, and only when he turned on Russia did we dare to hope. On the wireless Old Winnie goes growl and prevail, and then they play God Save the King.

~~~

Their mother's older brother, Uncle Fritz, has become an American soldier, and he arrives in uniform to see them. "It's amazing, isn't it," he tells the boys, "how much I've grown," and laughs at his own witticism and brings a goose and bottle of sherry and a large box of chocolates because he has no ration book; "I am a cornucopia," he says.

They celebrate reunion and look at the photograph album Fritz carries and talk about the family and how their parents are. "My, my," says Julia, "aren't you elegant in this uniform," and he says he had to change his name in order to be in the army, not Fritz any longer but Fred.

"Fred?"

Tall and fair, he blushes, his skin suffusing pinkly and his eyes bright blue. "Well, I didn't have to do it, but it makes everything simpler in the American army, and afterwards for business. It will be better with this name; you must come to visit," he says. "The land of opportunity."

"Where the streets are paved with gold," says Karl. "Apparently."

The brother and sister walk and talk and laugh in unfeigned intimacy and he tells her everything about their parents, Omi and Opi, and how he and his family manage. His other grandparents, Ben knows, have escaped from Germany—such stories I could tell you—and are already in America but went to Cuba first. "'Oh brave new world, that hath such creatures in it,'" says Uncle Fritz. "It *is* a brave new world."

"In my opinion," says Elsa, "Shakespeare is better in German; the Schlegel brothers are *mehr Shakespeare als Shakespeare.*"

"Be that as it may," says Julia, and then they finish the wine. But then Fritz has to leave again, for his has been a weekend pass, and he will see them soon.

"Very soon?" she asks.

"I promise, yes, as soon as ever possible."

"*Ach*, my blue-eyed soldier," Julia says, "I miss you very much."

"Imagine," she tells Ben afterwards, "I spent my childhood with him every day, the way you do with Jacob, and now I see him once a year and there's an ocean between us. But he says the end is coming and the end is near."

***

"What is this letter?"

"A."

"What is *this* letter?"

"C."

"What does this word spell, can you spell it?"

"Bessie, I'm a little messy," he tells Jacob, and his brother says, "Don't be silly," and he tells him, "Silly-billy," and then they play King of the Castle and then they all fall down.

The brothers have a cousin, Elizabeth-Anne. Gustave and Steffi's only daughter, she's "the child of their old age." This is their grandmother's expression; her parents are older than yours are, Elsa says, and little Elizabeth is younger than you, and therefore she's the child of their old age. On the platform of the Hampstead tube their cousin cries so much Ben tells her, "Silly-billy, don't you cry." In the bottom of the tube, he says, it's safe and people get to sleep here if they have a house where bombs dropped down or if they never had a shelter of their own.

"Except," Jacob asks, "what if a bomb dropped to the platform with the lift, or came down the stairway behind us; then what?"

"Bombs aren't intelligent enough to take the lift," Paul interrupts. "Let's go and fetch the eggs."

They have seven chickens, and Benjamin can count them: "One and two and three." Then, *"Four and five and six."*

He can count up to one hundred and do his sums, but Elizabeth can't; she's just a silly-billy, he says, a girl with dirty knickers. Where are your manners, his grandmother asks, where's my chevalier? King George goes walking every day out among his people with an umbrella and bids them be of good cheer; Queen Mary says my lovely London, and she means it too. But today when Paul and Ben go outside to the coop the screen door hangs slackly open, giving out upon vacuity. The door creaks and squeaks on its hinge. A single chicken roosts within, preening, imperturbable, and they look in the bedding for eggs.

"But that's terrible," says Julia, when the boy runs to the kitchen with the burden of discovery. "Wait till your father hears."

"We'll find them," Paul announces. "They can't be very far away; they can only fly a little and won't have traveled far."

"Was it a fox?" asks Julia.

"No, carelessness," he says.

So they look everywhere for chickens, and Paul catches two. They find them just across the street, hard by the place the hedgehog sleeps, and Paul collects them, clucking, and they walk back to the coop. Then Benjamin fastens the door latch securely and they begin to look at Mrs. Plimsoll's house, and there's a chicken in a tree and he gets to rattle the food in his cup, the corn shells and peelings, until it too comes down. Elizabeth-Anne comes out to help, but she can't catch a chicken, he tells her, and she runs around the lawn and falls and goes inside crying.

"Good riddance to bad rubbish."

"Don't say that," says Paul, but he's laughing.

"Good riddance to bad rubbish," Benjamin repeats.

And so they go around the corner and everywhere they call out *chickychicky* here *chickychicky* and are looking in particular for hens. The boy is standing underneath the monkey tree, the one he walks to on his nature walks, and up there there's a broody hen and it commences to rain. Then he hears the siren, the large horn blaring *poopoowha*, until his companion comes running and they run back to the house. This time, Ben learns, it's not a bomb and not a plane and nothing bad, and his mother doesn't care what's in the tree and his father's on the telephone and calling from the office because the sirens mean the war is over and we won, he's coming home.

IV

Benjamin: 1946

"SHE CAN'T STAY by herself," says Daddy. "She really can't
manage alone."

"I know."

"She must be watched."

"That much at least is obvious."

"But we don't have the room," he says. "Not really."

"Gustave does," says Mummy.

"*Doch.*"

"Will he take her?"

"At least to begin with. We'll see."

They are talking about Granny and the place she has
to move. They say she fell down yesterday two times on
her walk. It isn't a question of balance so much as attention, says Daddy, it's only a question of taking it slowly
and using her cane on the steps. She used to live in Litch-
field Way but now it isn't possible, she simply can't stay
by herself. Except it *is* hard to imagine, Mummy tells him,

65

how she'll manage in the household since the first thing your grandmother complained about was how the room in Gustave's house is not as big or well appointed even as the bathroom she provided in the old days to the third upstairs maid. Well, that is the case, says Daddy, but she was complaining already, says Mummy, ten minutes after arrival, and it might not work. That's true enough, his father says, we'll see how things develop and how she can adjust. "We'll see," he says again, "*doch, doch,*" and Mummy says, "It's cold in here," and pulls the window down.

But when they say "We'll see," this time his parents don't mean yes, I promise, what they mean is just a minute, and we have to help her move. It's her eyes, they tell him when he asks, it's serious but not too serious and what Granny wants is company and somebody to stay with her, you can understand that can't you, *selbstverständlich,* Mister Blister, she gets lonely in the night.

"But she could sleep with Rafi."

"No. Not in the garage."

So they help her move to Gustave's up the stairs. In Hamburg, his grandmother tells him, we gave the maids adequate room. And I wouldn't give this bedroom for a water closet to the third upstairs maid. You are my chevalier, she says, and then she takes Ben's hand. She is losing her eyesight, she says, and this means she has to hold his hand and also keep her balance, and for a person who has used her eyes to look at scenery and flowers and masks and pictures all her life it isn't easy, there is *Sittlichkeit* and *Sinnlichkeit,* she says. *Ach,* such is life, she says.

Gustave's house is big and brick with a green fence in front of it; the gate swings open when you push hard against the iron ring. So finally she moves from her own flat to her son's house in Lyndhurst Road, the older part of Hampstead, and Daddy tells him that it will be better you'll see. His cousin Elizabeth-Anne sleeps just across the hall, and Steffi's mother Mrs. Feingold lives there also, so there are two old ladies, Granny says. What a household, Mummy says.

In her room his granny keeps a box of chocolate for him, and she smokes. She wears gray on Monday, Wednesday, Friday, Sunday and black on the three days between. When she smokes he watches the cigarette tip and how the ash gets long and falls and what it does to her dress. On the gray dress you can't see the ash but on the black you can. She has ashtrays on the table where she puts the cigarette, but when she sits to smoke she doesn't see the ashtray and she says it doesn't matter because the maid will clean. The maid must do *something*, she says. Then she offers him a *himbersaft* and she herself pours out a schnapps.

Himbersaft means raspberry syrup and he pours it in three ways. The first way is at the bottom of the glass, and then you add water and stir. The other way is put water in first and then you add the *himbersaft* and watch it trickle down. But the third way is his favorite; you put in water, just a little, then some *himbersaft* and then water again and you watch the layers shifting while you stir. "*The Consolations of Philosophy*," says Granny. "Did you know that book was written while its author was in jail?" He doesn't know, he answers, watching the syrup, and she says *ach, ja*, he languished in a prison cell, did great Boethius. It is not unlike this room, she says, and then she lights a cigarette, and when Ben asks her what she means by that she tells him such is life.

━━━⌒

Jacob gets to wear gray flannels and a coat and go to the King Alfred School and wear a cap. He has a badge on his coat. He says well it's hard work at a proper school and wait till you try it, you'll see. But Benjamin can go to Miss Jamaiker's and walk past the hedgehog and stay until lunchtime, and sometimes Mummy and sometimes Granny and Kathleen the maid come to fetch and walk him home. Kathleen the maid arrived from County Kerry in Ireland, and her uniform is green, and she got glass in her thumb. When she's red-faced and unhappy it's because of the glass in her thumb. Mummy says it hurts her once a month; once a month she has a temper fit and there's nothing left to do except wait for the glass to stop hurting, it causes her to bleed and you better stay out of the way. Can I see it, *can* I? he asks, and Kathleen tells him no. But once he saw her suck her thumb and when he asked her if it hurt she told him no, not now.

They take their nature walk on different streets since Granny moved to Gustave's house, and sometimes they go to the heath. On the heath they visit Johnny Weiser, who lives in the Vale of Health. They go up and down dancing together but he tells the boy Mister Blister you are getting sizable you'll dance soon enough by yourself. Watch this, Ben tells him, and lifts his arms like swimmabimma when Granny showed him how, and everybody laughs and claps and then he takes a bow.

So now he knows the book by heart and can read *Henry's Green Wagon* out loud. When he does the part about the paint and Bessie, *I'm a little messy,* he puts out his hands and shakes them as though there were green paint on top and everybody claps. Because it's nicest when they laugh at you and say what a performer, *entzückend,* good enough to eat. At Gustave's house they go for Sunday lunch and Granny steps down the staircase carefully, carefully one piece of stair with both feet at a time while he holds her and pulls out her chair and pushes in her chair and then she sits at the table and says, Well, what happened to the cheese? At Gustave's house there are Staffordshire figures, which are gentlemen built out of china and leaning on pianos or ladies with fans; there are sailors and soldiers and princes and rose-cheeked maidens everywhere, and Daddy calls them *kitsch.* Well I know that, Gustave says, but it's just a hobby, isn't it, the way you like Lautrec. But Toulouse is a wonderful artist, says Daddy, an excellent draftsman, so skillful, and besides he makes me laugh. I also, Gustave says, *Ich auch,* that's just how I feel about Staffordshire figures, I find them amusing, he says.

There are milkmaids and farmers and cows. There are ladies in hoop skirts and offering apples and sitting on rope swings, smiling; their chevaliers wear swords. They are everywhere in Lyndhurst Road, on the sideboard and the walls and in the cabinets, and also he has naked ladies by Rodin. But these little statues are excellent, says Daddy, can't you tell the difference? and Ben nods his head and promises he can. Except the ladies by Rodin have smudges all over their body and are built out of bronze; they lift their legs or curl their necks like the idea of dancers, says his father, can you see? Imagine that you're dancing and the sculptor watches and invites you to his house perhaps and then you take off all your clothes and he plays with clay. You can see the spot right here, right here, where Rodin put his thumb.

Ach, furchtbar, Granny says to him, *mein Sohn* where is your judgment, what are you telling the boy?

When he plays with Jacob on the coal they take turns on the top of the pile. First he has it then his brother has it and they get to throw not at each other, never at each other, but into the scuttle and they keep on throwing in until it bounces out. I'm the King of the Castle, and you're the dirty rascal, is the song they sing when throwing, and Jacob gets eight in a row. His brother is a lefty and he throws with his left hand; Ben throws instead with his right hand because more people are right-handed, Dr. Samson says, and he gets six in a row.

When the scuttle is full they must take it inside, and Kathleen doesn't have to, because of the glass in her thumb. We are going to America on holiday, says Mummy, and we will see Omi and Opi and my brother Fritz. We are going there this summer on a ship and we will visit everybody and examine where they live. Mummy sits and smokes a cigarette and tells Ben he is, yes, of course, the apple of her eye. But she stares out the window at where they keep chickens, where Jacob practices cricket, and when her Mister Blister asks her what's the matter she says nothing really, and she shakes her head. But come sit on my lap, Mummy says.

There is music on the gramophone: Beethoven's "Moonlight Sonata," which is her favorite. She strokes his hair and says he needs a haircut soon, her Goldilocks, and then she says, oh, Ben-Ben, it's a mystery, and when he asks her what she means she says the existence of evil, how a nation that can produce such music also made a Hitler. How is it possible, she says, that Bach and Brahms and Beethoven and Mozart—all of them—were part of such a culture? Robert Schumann and Franz Schubert too. And she turns her face to the wall. And the boy asks what's the matter, what's the matter but must try to understand, she tells him, how difficult it seems sometimes to know that where you once belonged is a country you will never see and cannot dream of visiting again.

"But we *could*," he tells her.

"No."

"If we wanted to . . ."

"I don't. I will never go to Germany again. They call it *Vaterland*, not *Mutterland*, do you understand the difference?"

"Yes."

"And when a whole country is evil like that it's madness to think of returning. Not ever."

"Do you miss it?"

"Yes," she says. "I miss it very much."

And then she gives him chocolate, and they sit and rock.

~

His father plays the cello and Paul plays the piano and Dr. Lucas brings a violin and Johnny Weiser a viola, and they come and drink a schnapps and then they fix the chairs and music stands and then they play. The four of them make music in the house. Jacob gets to turn the pages by the piano bench and stand right next to Paul, who nods his head, and Jacob turns and nods his head and taps his foot so Johnny Weiser says *ach ja* my boy, if you want to you can turn for me, just wait until I nod. But he doesn't know how to read music, says Jacob, and Ben tells him dirty rascal, and Dr. Lucas says all right, let's try the second movement, together *noch einmal* with the repeats. From B.

Then they start to play and Daddy tells him, winking, I'm best at the slow parts, I like it better *langsam*, but Johnny Weiser bends and rocks and nods his head at every measure when he's playing, each time he moves his bow, so Ben doesn't understand when he's supposed to turn. But this is Mozart, says Dr. Lucas, it isn't march music my boy. *Also, noch einmal,* from B. And Johnny says just wait till I tell you and he stands by Mr. Weiser's side and waits. Granny comes to their house for the concert and sits there on the sofa, her glasses on a ribbon chain, her eyes half-closed, always smoking, and he sees the ash drop down and Mummy sits there smoking too but she uses an ashtray instead. What a genius, sighs Dr. Lucas, what an astonishing genius; and so young at the time, and Daddy asks, do you know, Ben, that Wolfgang Amadeus Mozart and Felix Mendelssohn-Bartholdy were composing at your age already? and so he turns the page.

But what about the poet Goethe? Daddy says. Johann Wolfgang von Goethe was a universal genius; he understood government just as much as poetry; his work on color theory is absolutely first-rate. There is nothing in the language to equal Faust, Part One. Well, parts of Part Two also, but *Gretchen am Spinnrade*, he says, what music in that verse. *"Meine Ruh' ist hin, mein Herz ist schwer,"* he says, his eyes closed, and the others chorus, *"Ich finde sie nimmer und nimmermehr."* And he also understood, says Dr. Lucas, milkmaids and Lotte in Weimar; *Dans la présence des enfants,* Granny says, in this house we don't discuss such things, not while I sit and listen to them, please.

All right then, I apologize, he says. But I was only remarking on the similarity between Mozart and Goethe in this case; they both had a great appetite for life. Speaking of which, says Johnny Weiser, I myself have a great appetite; I worked so hard in that scherzo I must have a sandwich at least. And also *etwas zu trinken,* thank you, Julia, a glass of your good red wine.

It is not Mozart and Goethe, says Dr. Lucas, but Beethoven and Schiller I think of so often together, with that brilliant Ode to Joy. Oh stop it, stop it, Mummy says, they would all of them have been Nazis, they would every single one of them have joined the party, if given half the chance. With the single exception of Heine. And he only because he was Jewish and would not have been permitted to join; *Entschuldigen Sie,* says Dr. Lucas, but I do not agree. There is art and there is politics, and even if they sometimes mix they are in essence separate; what is this? Johnny Weiser asks. Where do you find such Stilton, it is excellent. As a general rule, he explains, the English are not famous for their cheese, but that is a mistake, because a first-rate Stilton or a Cheshire is as good as what you find these days from France. It will be a long long time before the production of cheese again, or adequate export of wine. On Tavistock Hill, says Mummy, at the cheese shop there. Shall we begin again? asks Daddy. I myself feel quite refreshed.

Outside it rains. The boy watches the rain at the window, the way the raindrops splatter on the pane and how they fall and hold the glass and then slip down it, diving. Kathleen has pulled the curtains to, but not completely, and at the bottom of the pane the curtains rise and wave and in between the strip of window glass is like a mirror or a river where you watch the water gather, this way, that way, this way, that, and then divide and drip. *Also, noch einmal,* says Dr. Lucas, from C.

So Jacob turns the page for Paul and Johnny Weiser whispers, *now,* and then he smiles at Benjamin and they continue with the Mozart and Granny smiles and waves her cigarette in its cigarette holder, unlit. Will you play the violin, she asks, or the viola or your father's cello, which instrument do you prefer? The men have hung their jackets up and play in their shirtsleeves and ties; Johnny Weiser's shirt is wet, and Carla Weiser says you can't imagine how much he sweats or how often he has to change shirts. Profusely, she declares. Dr. Lucas wears suspenders the same color as his tie; he is a dandy, Mummy tells the boy, a regular Beau Brummel but it would be much better if he could play in tune. This is, he thinks, our family, this lamplit circle in the living room, and *Kammermusik* means chamber music and the living room's a chamber now because we have no music room. In Hamburg and Berlin there was a room set aside especially for music, both his parents lived in houses that were much bigger than this. But we're alive and very fortunate, says Mummy, Mister Blister, are we not?

⌒

"Shall we go walking?" Granny asks.

"It's raining," Ben tells her.

"Will you melt?"

"No."

"Are you made out of sugar?"

"No."

"Then let's take our nature walk."

His mother says be careful, *vorsicht*, but if you want to and you're careful it's all right. Granny takes her cane and hat with the black veil and little black dots on the net and he walks beside her to the hedge at Miss Jamaiker's school, and then they go through it and look for the hedgehog, but Granny can't see it asleep. It is just at the foot of the tree where he points but personally I must look with my mind's eye, she says. I see what I have seen before and close my eyes, remembering, but you, my little chevalier, have a great deal to learn for the first time instead. What do you see *zum Beispiel,* she asks, when you look at that building there?

"Miss Jamaiker's."

"No."

"My school."

"No. I asked you what you see," she says.

"The place they teach me numbers. The place I am learning to read."

"Not really."

"So what, then?"

"You see a white wall. You see a red shape that's the door inside the white shape that we call a wall and then some black where there are windows; you see color only, and matters of proportion."

"It's Miss Jamaiker's," he says.

"No, that's what you decide," she says. "And what we've taught you to call it. Not what you see but what it means."

"All right."

"And when it's what it means," she says, "your eye's not any longer innocent."

"I didn't know you wanted me to tell you only color . . ."

"The innocent eye," Granny tells him again. "It's in Boethius," she tells him. "Such is life."

                       *

They are going to America but he doesn't want to go. They are taking a ship that will last eleven days and is a freighter, Jacob tells him, because the other ships still carry troops. Troops are soldiers going home. It is only for a visit but you will be seasick, he says. What's seasick? the boy asks, and his brother says when you can't stand on land and are dizzy and throw up and hate it, he says; you will hate it, I wager. Sailing sailing over the bounding main, he says, but Benjamin will throw up awfully and not go home again.

Have you been there? he asks Granny, and she tells him *furchtbar,* no. What is America? he asks, and Jacob says it's the revolting colonies but Mummy says where Uncle Fritz has gone to live, and where my parents are. It's a business trip, says Daddy, because it's a major market for bristles and horsehair and we have no office there. Johnny Weiser thinks I ought to go and establish a branch of the firm in New York, and so does Henry Meyer, and in any case I'll make the trip and thought it would be fun for everyone to come along. Don't you worry, Mister Blister, it will be an adventure you'll see.

Where he hides is on the heath. They are all at Johnny Weiser's house, and it's a fine spring day, he says, why don't the boys play outside. Not long, says Mummy, not too long, we have to be going, she says. Henry Meyer isn't feeling well; his face is white and he sits with a blanket on his shoulders and another on his knees. His face is wet; he smells. When Henry Meyer came to Hamburg he said, Karl, listen, you get out of here, just pay the exit tariff and send me as much furniture as possible, just take what you can and come across to England; if you wait a little longer even it will be too late. It was twenty-five percent last month, and next month it will be forty, and soon it will be eighty and then ninety, *und so weiter.* And he was right about the tariff, Daddy says, and now if he asks me to go to America I must oblige him and discharge my obligation. Because we owe him everything, if he hadn't said come work with me I wouldn't be alive. But it will be an adventure and we will come back, Mister Blister, of course, and you and Jacob run outside and come back in twenty minutes; take your coats.

What is seasick? he asks Jacob, and his brother says well close your eyes and twirl around and twirl around ten times. Then pretend you ate a plate of worms and turn ten times again. How do you know? Ben asks him, and he says Geoffrey Kell was seasick on only the channel and he told me all about it and so was Robert Elkeles and you will feel it too. Well I'm not going anyhow, the boy declares and then he runs away.

His brother follows but he keeps on running until Jacob chasing him is shouting good riddance to bad rubbish, and then he hides behind a bush and Jacob can't find him anywhere because he holds his breath. His brother shouts oh all right then I'm sorry, but Benjamin stays hidden, swallowing, until his brother says I mean it cross my heart I didn't really mean it and then he counts to ten. When his brother leaves he keeps his eyes tight shut because it is raining, he's not made out of sugar, but Jacob is bad rubbish and Ben will not melt. Except he can hear a dog bark. There is bark like the bark of a tree and growl and howl and whine and wine and bark.

They are going to America but he hides on the heath. If they find him they will make him go; if they leave he'll stay with Robin Hood and Friar Tuck and all the merry men or live in Granny's room in Gustave's house or perhaps on the third floor there up under the roof and he thinks they must be missing me, they will be sorry when I'm gone. So he runs to Johnny Weiser's before anybody finds him but in the wrong direction, and the place he ran from Jacob is not easy now to find; the trees are enormous; they hiss. A yellow dog resolves itself, approaching, from the component parts of dusk and, *Nacht und Nebel,* darkness, fog. What he wants now awfully is just to be with everyone, and when his father whistles Schubert it comes as a relief. Well there you are, Karl tells the boy, come along now, Mister Blister, and again again he's home.

V

Elsa: 1946

SHE SITS IN THE ONE CHAIR. She regards a stone Khmer head and a face by Käthe Kollwitz on the wall above it; there is a certain similarity of attitude in the expression of the Kollwitz woman and on the ancient visage, its half-smile, its curved lip. What *is* there, Elsa asks herself, about such focused staring that compels her own present attention: the level glare, the etched arched eyebrow or the eye without a pupil gazing from its oval at her blankly? The eyes or the edge of the mouth?

Upon the oak end table at her right side stands a full decanter and a brushed silver cigarette box. She feels for a cigarette, lights it, then lets the match fall to the carpet and puts her foot on the match. Inhaling, she shuts her left eye. Downstairs she can discern the bustle of arrival, first the sound of the car door and doorbell and footsteps, next the high-pitched hum of greetings, and knows therefore that Karl and Julia and their two boys have come and soon her little Benjamin will start running up the steps. He will knock on her locked door, her chevalier, and she will say, "Come in." Beyond, sunshine is streaming and she welcomes it: sky visible, an elm tree at the window and a bluebird on the branch. Exhaling, she awaits his approach: such is life.

It is 1946, and she plays her memory game. As always he will ask his questions and, as always, she will answer. Can you remember ten years back? I can. Can you remember twenty? *Doch*, but fifty years? *Gewiss*. In 1896 your grandfather proposed to me, although of course he signaled his intentions to my father long before. My own father would have been willing, but it was a delicate matter because my father's partner, the principal of S. R. Levi Company, had wanted your grandfather Ludwig to marry his daughter instead. She was cross-eyed and too fat. She was, I have to tell you, an unattractive person and not getting any younger, and your grandfather was her last chance. Ludwig worked, you understand, as an apprentice in the company; at that time he had been buying furs and his future was a bright one if he married properly, but not so bright if he did not, and I myself was too young. It had been Mr. Levi's intention that your grandfather marry his daughter, but this was not to be. He wished to marry me. And so when he came into the office and said, Sir, I request your permission, permission was not granted and we had to wait three years while he traveled for the company and earned off his apprenticeship and was promoted finally and came to the house, hat in hand.

I remember that hat: gray, a black silk strip around it, and the way he kept turning the brim. I remember how he looked at me, the two of us alone together in the corner of the sitting room, and how it would have been good manners to leave the hat along with his coat in the cloak room when he entered, but he just kept turning it around and around, and this was perhaps a way of saying that he too was nervous, not knowing how to proceed. I have done what I promised, he said, I have served out my apprenticeship and am now a junior partner and my prospects there are good. He was a modest man, your grandfather, he did not call them "excellent" but "good." In truth his business position was already an excellent one, because Robert Schwartz had died by then, and old Mr. Levi was too ill to come to the office for more than an hour every morning and sit at his desk and drink tea. And I told him that I also keep my promise and abide by it, *selbstverständlich*, self-evidently, and he said would you care for a walk?

It was very different then, it wasn't possible to do the things young people do today. Aunt Hella came along with us but at least she had the decency to stop and examine the flower beds while we two walked ahead. And now I come to think of it she had been in the sitting room also, she was knitting while he turned his hat, and only outside there did we have some privacy, which is the reason, *selbstverständlich*, we take our nature walks. Outside there you feel free. From the hillside up above the house we could see the harbor and there were many boats preparing for departure, because the wind had freshened, and your grandfather had just returned from sailing on the Baltic Sea on business to Russia so he understood the names of the sails and the way the helmsman must proceed and he

81

talked about it a very long time until I wanted to say, finally, this is enough. But I was very nervous, not to say preoccupied and wondering what I should say, and now I know he had been nervous also which is why he talked about navigation and the arrangement of the tiller and the sails. Because what he was planning to do was also a departure, a thing he'd had no practice for until up there he removed his hat and turned to me with such a sweet expression and said, Elsa, might I ask you for a kiss?

I looked around for Aunt Hella; she was making a bouquet. She had given us her back. It is fifty years ago but I remember it clearly: the clouds, the wind, a dog on a leash, the feel of his whiskers upon my own cheek when I presented it, and then the first touch of his lips. There is *Sittlichkeit* and *Sinnlichkeit,* correct? My father and my uncles were the only men who'd kissed me, you must understand, and also once a cousin on a picnic, but none of it was serious and everything was unimportant until that day above the harbor where we agreed to marry and he offered me this ring. Not once since then in fifty years — not for the bath or shower stall, not in the hospital, not in my final pregnancy when I delivered your father and my body kept its water and became, so to say, enormous — never for a single instant have I removed this ring. Not for anything else that the world has to offer would I take it off this finger, and when I die you must bury it too. There is much I cannot remember on purpose and many years of suffering a person must try to dismiss. I have forgotten many things: some I forget in the course of events and others I choose to forget. But the white sails in the harbor and my sunshine man, my Ludwig, the hat in his hand and the expression on his face when he said, Elsa, will you marry me? —that day I will remember all my life.

———

"*Wie geht's*, Mama?"

"*Wie?*" She hears her son's key in the lock.

"The others have arrived," says Gustave. "We hope you will join us downstairs."

"He should have been a painter."

"Who?"

"Schicklgruber. I blame the art school. The directors behaved very foolishly."

"Permit me." Gustave has turned on the light.

"Because if they accepted him while he still hoped to paint we would have had to look at only poor portraits and second-rate still-lifes and landscape. But not this madness, these atrocities."

"Mama, would you enjoy some tea?"

"*Wie?*"

"Tea," he says, more loudly.

"If we stay here the whole winter, I am obliged to ask why did we leave Hamburg in the first place?"

"We were forced to, remember? It wasn't our choice."

"No. And not my preference . . ."

"I'll let you rest a little, then."

"*Ganz gern*," she says. "With pleasure."

"But soon I'll send up Benjamin. He will help you with the stairs." And, leaving, her son shuts the door.

"My chevalier," she says.

Now finishing her cigarette, she deposits it into the ash-tray and empties her glass and stands up. She straightens the sleeve at her wrist. Her own room must be always locked or they will come inside to clean and, if she is not careful, steal; they pretend it is to dust and wash the sheets and bring along the carpet sweeper in order to rub out the cigarette ash. Ash is good for the carpet, Elsa main-tains, and she could open the windows and close them again by herself. Except, Madame, replies the maid, you shouldn't have to occupy yourself with carpet sweeping, and in every other room of the house, for example Mrs. Feingold's, my job here is to clean.

But she lost her carved ivory camel last week, and she herself is certain the Irish maid or Steffi's mother took it. There were eleven cigarettes inside the box, and now she can only count six. Mrs. Feingold has the room next door, and they share a bathroom and heartily detest each other, do they not: Steffi's mother, *that old cow*. Rachel Feingold had hoped to be an actress; she had a great personal love of the theater, if one believes the things she says, but in the period when she was young no respectable girl could make a career as actress, and so she complied with her family's wishes and did not pursue life on stage. Yet she had been theatrical—or so she assures anyone who will listen—with an excellent voice for singing and a flair for performance and entertainment, and she likes to boast about herself as someone young and sprightly and doing the can-can in Paris or the city her family hailed from, Nuremberg.

Elsa does not believe it, of course. The ancient, shriveled woman in the room beside her could not have been a dancer of any consequence; more likely once or twice she attended the theater or ballet and made of this a big affair, with her habit of exaggeration that continues to this day. When Elsa descends to join them at mealtimes they come tiptoeing upstairs instead and remove her cigarettes and matches and the ivory camel and bottle of schnapps; they take advantage of her, all of them, they believe she isn't watching since her eyesight has grown poor. They put their fingers on the Kollwitz and smudge the stone Khmer head.

In her pocket therefore she keeps a ring of keys, and now she locks the door again until her grandson appears. Gustave requires a spare second set. What if you're locked inside and you should need me? he asks. Let us say you have a fall, or there's a problem with the faucet, or perhaps you don't feel well at night and ring the bell for help? It's reasonable, is it not, to have another key?

She could not deny this; she has denied him nothing, nothing, and he therefore keeps a set of keys for the purposes of rescue and gives them to Feingold the cow. Well, perhaps he does not offer them precisely; he leaves them hanging in the garden room and Steffi and the maid and Mrs. Feingold remove them from the hook and come and take her cigarettes or, in the process of changing her sheets, take a swallow from the bottle or a piece of Toblerone chocolates near and dear to her in this her single refuge and only private space. In Hamburg, she tells Benjamin, she would not have given such a room to the third upstairs maid.

And it was true; her people were well treated, they had nothing to complain about in wages or treatment or food. Lotte Pulfermacher treated her own maids, by comparison, scandalously, without the slightest kindness, and never let her staff forget that they could be replaced. *Quod licet Jovi, non licet bovi,* Lotte used to say. That which Jove can do a cow cannot; what is permitted to the gods the cattle have no license for. Lotte said this often, *Quod licet Jovi,* and did not need to finish the sentence before it was clear what she meant: this maid will be replaced.

You have holes in your dresses, Mama, Steffi says; your pockets do not keep the keys, often they fall from your pockets. Not to mention cigarettes. Not to mention what you do with matches and the risk of fire in your bed. And we do not want to make you feel as if you have no privacy; we have no intention of searching your room, but we do need to enter it upon occasion for the cleaning. That's all there is to it, she says. It is not a topic for discussion, really; we have taken off the deadbolt and have made a second set and you needn't think about it but as the lady of the house I must insist.

So now that she stays in the house of her children she, Elsa, has no choice. It is *shrecklich,* it is *Wahnsinn,* and if her husband were alive they would not dare to speak such slanders to her face. But he is not alive, her lovely sunshine chevalier and gallant husband Ludwig; he died in Schicklgruber's country of a cancer in the lungs. Only once did he complain. Only once when the doctors had failed to arrive, and when at last they did arrive and tardily, carelessly gave him his shot, before he drifted into sleep he said to her, *Ach,* Elsa, they would not be half so careless if they came here for a loan. Or for your famous Sunday breakfast; they would always have been prompt. On my birthday we would always have the first asparagus, remember? he asked, the young bright green asparagus in season, and also a plate of fresh eggs.

Then he lay back on the pillows, smiling faintly, smiling painfully, and said, *Schatz,* you must let a man sleep.

She herself is not so patient; she calls Mrs. Feingold "cow." She has threatened the maid with her cane. She should not have done it, perhaps, but there are limits to her patience and she has tried very hard and many times to be polite. On the second floor they all live together, with the child Elizabeth in the third back bedroom, and it is peculiar how they manage: the parents and the two old ladies and one girl. Because the little Elizabeth is being raised with impossible manners; she does not wipe her lips before she drinks, and the difference between spoon and fork is, to her, a mystery. Gustave pays her no attention and Steffi is too busy with her charity cases in Golders Green. When Elizabeth clatters down the staircase to the breakfast room she grumbles; when she talks to her parents she shrieks. One must love each of the grandchildren equally, *natürlich,* but this one will be difficult and it takes no crystal ball to see the future will be hard for her, the way that she is growing up without any manners at all.

"Oh Granny," she says, "it's a bother," and if they take a nature walk she says, "Granny it's only a tree . . ."

Now, twice, her grandson knocks. He has arrived at her door. They are going to America on holiday; they will take a steamship out of Liverpool and therefore they have come to say goodbye. It is only on holiday—business also—

since Karl does what his father did, traveling for import-export and returning with what you call a *cadeau:* a kilo of Russian caviar or box of first-rate tea. *This* one is her special companion and although a grandmother should not have such opinions, it is her opinion that he will become someone special, for this one now, this Benjamin—"Just a minute," she calls out to him, "Just a minute, *Augenblick*"—has proper manners already and such a happy smile.

The room adjusts. It moves to her left as she moves to the right; it is like a dancing partner in the old days at a dance. Above the windswept harbor he took his hat into his hands and, turning the brim, modest, smiling, said, *Schatz,* you must let a man sleep.

～⌒

Benjamin enters. "Hullo," she says.

"Hello, Granny."

"Don't you look smart," she says. "What a shirt."

"Do you like it?"

"*Natürlich.* The color goes well with your eyes."

"Mummy bought it for me yesterday. She says I get to wear a tie like Daddy's with this shirt."

"When?"

"On the boat."

"*Das Boot,*" she says. "*Das Schiff.*"

"It's called a freighter, Jacob says. And he says I'll be seasick."

"*Übel* just a little maybe, which *auf Englisch* they call queasy. But only the first day."

"'Oh the life of a sailor is hard, me hearties, the life of a sailor is hard.'"

"And what is that?"

"A song my brother knows."

"Is he downstairs?"

"Yes, everybody is. They sent me to fetch you for tea."

"But do you like this elephant?" She has prepared a *cadeau.*

"They're waiting, Granny. There's scones."

"Do you see this shiny part on the top of the elephant's head?"

"Yes."

"That's where he's rubbed for good luck. That's where we pat him when we're feeling *übel* or frightened."

"And Sacher torte," he tells her. "And lemon cake and cheese."

"I want you to have it."

"Right now?"

"Yes. And then to bring it back to me when you yourself return."

—————

So she gathers up her cane and shawl and magnifying glass and together they descend the stairs, she leaning on Benjamin's arm. There are twenty-three separate treads, and Elsa has memorized the procedure, eleven with a banister, and then a little turnaround, and twelve stairs with a banister to the entrance hall. In this manner when she commences she stands above but to the right-hand side of the spot where she will finish, and often she pauses on the landing where there are books and a window, halting to gather herself for the descent's further progress and survey the scene below. One must make an entrance; one must understand the room.

Below is her family, laughing. To her eyes they make a jumbled mass, a welter of inconstant shape, a puzzle of color in motion, and she listens to single them out. Little Benjamin stands close beside her, his hand on her elbow, *entzückend*. Without raising her glass she can see to the right the flowers by Schmidt-Rottluff and the self-portrait by Kirchner that she had given to Gustave when he first left the house in Hamburg, as a way of saying *bon voyage*, as an inducement to remember his home and what you call a *cadeau*. The red rose goes well with the blue. The vase Schmidt-Rottluff painted was a vase she used to own. The ring on her finger is one he designed, with her initials incised upon an oval silver disc. It is not as dear to her as Ludwig's ring, the one she never would remove, but it is admirable nevertheless and as she lifts her left hand to the banister she catches the glint of it, winking.

Then they continue down the stairs slowly past Staffordshire figures, a shield from the Sepic River and two Josef Herman watercolors of men pitching hay in a field. There is a naked lady by Pascin and also one by Rodin; *gestern* she instructed her son to remove them from the stairwell but he told her it was not a problem for anyone else; it was less particular, he said, than *Gray's Anatomy*, and anyhow his daughter soon enough would need to study herself and see the difference in a mirror between her own young body and the girl by Pascin or Rodin. Now for the time being ignore it, Mama, now leave it alone on the wall.

There sit Gustave and Steffi and Elizabeth-Anne and Mrs. Feingold the cow. They look up at her, unsmiling, impatient to eat. "*Endlich,*" Mrs. Feingold says. "*Finalmente,*" says her son, "so now we all can start." There are Karl and Julia, her daughter-in-law, his clever wife, and standing by the sideboard now, both Benjamin and Jacob: the ones who will go to America and leave her here alone. It is a party to wish them safe journey and Godspeed and safe return.

"Do you want a little soup, Mama?" asks Steffi.

"Yes. All right."

"Will you join us at the table, then?"

"What kind of soup?"

"My mushroom and barley. The kind that you like."

"*Ein Tässchen, bitte.* Just one cup."

"Good," Steffi says, and serves.

Behind her hangs a large Peter Paul Rubens—an oil depicting Phaeton's fall—which Gustave found in an estate sale and recognized as real; the horses in particular are excellent, and the torso of the sun-doomed hero plunging from the chariot. The cabinet holds Staffordshire: a gentleman playing the piano while a pink-cheeked maiden sings. Each of the piano keys is visible and gleaming beneath the pianist's hands. There is a statue of the Duke of Wellington, standing upright in a martial pose, his hand upon the pommel of his sword. There is a sailor with an eye patch modeled on Admiral Nelson, holding up a telescope and sextant, and one with a peg leg. There is a plump Napoleon riding on a donkey, arms tied behind his back. "After Waterloo," the legend reads, and above the emperor's tricornered hat flies the Union Jack.

Lotte Pulfermacher has arrived, and also Dr. Samson, and Johnny and Carla Weiser will be coming any minute but they have not appeared as yet and we should begin. Punctuality, Elsa believes, is the politeness of kings. Boethius would never keep a beggar waiting, nor a prince, and the former was as hungry as the latter, often more. The prince could satisfy himself whenever he desired, but the beggar had to wait. Do they know the story of a beggar in Vienna who received a gift of *Groschen* from a charitable burgher passing by, and then two hours later the burgher found the man to whom he had given his charity eating salmon mayonnaise? At the Hotel Sacher, no less. And the rich man upbraided the poor one for his lack of seriousness, his failure in the savings and the self-control department and unwillingness to wait. So, said the beggar, when I have no money I cannot eat salmon mayonnaise. And when I do have money I may not eat salmon mayonnaise. In this case, will the gentleman inform me when should I eat my portion of salmon mayonnaise?

"Is that in Boethius?" Lotte asks, but she does not bother to answer; it cannot be found in Boethius, *selbstverständlich*, but in Sigmund Freud. When Boethius was writing from his prison cell in Rome there had been no Hotel Sacher, nor Demel's across the way, but human nature does not change; it is a constant, unfortunately, and now that she is old and poor she is the butt of jokes. To bear a slight with dignity is nobler in the mind than to trade insults with cattle; *quod licet Jovi,* she reminds the woman at her side, is not permitted to cows.

Now Elizabeth-Anne smacks her lips. Her napkin ring is tarnished and she bites her fingernails and when she finishes her cake she sucks her thumb.

"Explain it," Elsa says.

"What?"

"Why the family left Germany. Why Hitler did not go to art school."

"We had no choice, Mama," says Gustave.

"Himmler, Goebbels, Hermann Göring—the one with the good eye for pictures?" Addressing the table, she raises her fork. "The one who was an art collector, yes?"

"Yes, and what about him?"

"It was everybody, wasn't it, the guilty men, and all of them collecting . . ."

"Are you cold, Mama?"

"*Ach ja,* it was terribly cold there. But I am cold now always."

"Old age," Karl tells the table. "It is not always a blessing."

"Send me a postcard," Elsa says. "Where I go there are no postcards. Send me the news of your voyage."

"All right," says Julia. "Gladly."

"Where I myself am going, there is no mail to send." She nods, confirming this. "My little chevalier."

"'Oh the life of a sailor is hard,'" says Jacob, "'the life of a sailor is hard.'"

When she closes her eyes an instant it is all around her, everywhere, the hills above the harbor and their lingering embrace, then the ring on her finger, the hat in his hand, the little white dog on a leash. *Dearest I have waited for this moment, I have hoped for three years daily that it would arrive.*

93

Ben's knees are pink and yellow and, although his new striped shirt looks proper and smart, his socks are imperfectly white. But such is, she tells herself, life.

~~~

Elsa tastes her mushroom soup. The barley is sufficient but does require salt. When she looks for her elephant, later, the one that she gave Benjamin, and cannot find it anywhere she will accuse the maid. What Schicklgruber could not do, or the jealousy of rivals, what the death of her parents and sisters and friends and dear dear precious Ludwig and her ensuing solitude and those she quarreled with and those who quarreled with her could never quite accomplish—a yielding loss, an acknowledged defeat—will be nonetheless accomplished by the decades' span, the weight of years accreting and causing her to bow, to bend: *thy will be done.*

And therefore she stays in the house, declining. During such a century, of course, she cannot believe in the existence of God, the merciful God of the Gentiles or vengeful of the Jews, no spirit immanent in trees or white-bearded hovering presence in the clouds. Yet it is madness to assert or in behavior to pretend that nothing submits to the passage of time or that such alteration may be, if admitted, avoided. There are *Sinnlichkeit* and *Sittlichkeit,* the life of the body and life of the mind, and both of them will stay with her as half-remembered echo, a melody repeated if only out of habit, and in the minor key. And she will make excursions. She will enjoy a visit to Bournemouth in the heat of summer for a week or, this next season, a fortnight, rocking on the high veranda of the Regency Hotel and watching while the other guests engage in their activities, croquet and backgammon, swimming, flirtation—the chatter and display of barristers and office clerks, young people on their honeymoons or soldiers on home leave. She enjoys a trip in autumn to the Cotswolds or to Devon, if her son will drive. Often Gustave must visit a museum or an artist or collector, and he says he welcomes company and so she goes along. The world beyond her window is a white-rimmed shadow merely, a blur of color washed and leached, but this suffices as reminder, this is not nothing to see.

Once she herself was part of it, engaged by it—the dream of getting and spending, the bustle of desire—but now she sits apart from those who are ambitious and has the consolation of, if not philosophy, old age. Now even such excursions as an afternoon at Kenmore can make her feel accomplished, as though the narrow confines of her room have been expanded to a country house not five miles away at the edge of the heath, the sloping lawn and the prospect of trees, as though Rembrandt and Vermeer might speak to her, familiar, although she cannot see them now: *Guten Tag, Elsa, wie geht's* . . .

For her eighty-second birthday she will return to Italy, taking the waters at Montecatini and having one last look at Michelangelo's marbles in Florence and his high vaulted ceiling in Rome. It is, she knows, farewell. For her eighty-fifth she travels to the south of France, visiting the nephew of a second cousin her husband helped establish in the import and export of olive oil and wine and who owns a villa near Apt. He himself is no spring chicken any longer; he is childless and a widower and seventy-eight years old. He has excellent manners, however. He says, Elsa, you are welcome here, you are an honored visitor and I wish everything to be to your entire satisfaction; I owe your husband a great deal, my livelihood as well as life, his memory is green for me, and I very much feel gratified to see you sitting in my garden in the sun.

They take tea and biscuits together; they talk of the old days in Hamburg and the astonishment of motorcars and airplanes and what are today called satellites, how the Russians celebrate the triumph of their Sputnik and how the world has changed. For five years she travels to Apt every fall, enjoying the olive and fig trees and bone-swaddling heat of the sun. But although this has been pleasant and a source of satisfaction there are limits nevertheless; her balance is not what it should be, her desire to enter museums or peer at sights of local interest—the Roman roads, the Aqueduct and Amphitheater—disappears. *Zum Beispiel*, for example, she had been told that Boethius died in the region, and she hired a car and was driven to see the philosopher's tomb, but when she arrived it was the wrong Boethius—just a man of the church in a crypt. And she no longer finds amusing the spectacle of tourists, the girls wearing nothing but napkins, the boys with their hair in a braid.

Then her second cousin's nephew, George, has an operation on his leg in Apt, and when that fails to halt the cancer he has an amputation and now must sit in a wheelchair for hours, swallowing pills and pastis; he is unenthusiastic and sleeps much of the day. And so on her ninetieth birthday she renounces travel altogether and waits in her room in Lyndhurst Road for visitors instead.

They come. They continue to do so for years, bringing medicine and gossip and the news of Clement Attlee, Anthony Eden and Harold Macmillan and the one in the cardigan, Harold Wilson, all those men who run for office and make speeches and win elections and become Prime Minister and then are voted out. The English are quite serious; they take these matters seriously, and since she is grateful to England for its behavior in the war she tries to do the same, but it has grown more difficult for her to distinguish who's in, who's out or why. They make a fuss over Suez. Fat King Farouk is deposed. Elsa cannot remember, however, if it was Farouk or the equally fat Aga Khan who weighed himself against diamonds, receiving subjects' tribute on a great hanging scale. Because for someone to sit in a scale and receive the tribute of his impoverished subjects—balancing his weight by gold and pearls and rubies—is a provocation, surely, and it should not be surprising if there's trouble in Suez.

Her visitors arrive with regularity, and they tell her of the illnesses of politicians and friends. Aneurin Bevan dies. Winston Churchill dies. When President John F. Kennedy gets shot in Dallas, Texas, it is a madness, a *Wahnsinn*, the permission in America for everyone to purchase guns. Such a thing would not happen in England, she thinks, because of the absence of weapons, but although the papers say the young martyr was cut down in his prime it is just another example, *letzendlich*, of inevitable death; it would not have mattered, really, if his car was elsewhere or the top had been closed; he was *strahlend und fatal.* He was death-marked, finally, and nothing to be done.

Over time she loses weight. She loses interest in food, because she cannot taste it, and the distinction between mushroom soup and split pea soup with barley becomes, to her, unimportant; she can taste sugar in her tea and therefore she spoons in three helpings of sugar, but the rest of cuisine is a waste. Tobacco keeps its flavor still, or not so much its flavor as the flare and bite upon the tongue, and since this is true also for schnapps she smokes and drinks with pleasure or, if not pleasure, satisfaction. From her window in the winter months the distinction between night and day, the quarter and three-quarter moon, is not easy to establish, not so much a function of the dusk as a line drawn in pastel shakily: now the world wakes, now it sleeps.

For if life be a picture surrounded by the narrow edge of what had seemed expansive once, what Elsa sees each morning—spreading raspberry or strawberry or gooseberry or lingonberry jam on toast, using the silver-handled knife with her initials embossed, the platter chipped but not broken, not needing to be thrown away—is an image of impending dissolution, the body gone, the rest is dross, what thou lovest well remains. Her son's friend Elias Canetti remarked as much last time he came to visit, in his blue suit and dark blue vest and coming up the stairs to say, politely, how do you do. The two men were engaged, as always, in their earnest disputation, with her son's blithe dismissal of language and Canetti's also blithe but opposite conviction that words themselves do matter and the way he had of circling his teacup's rim with a wet finger till it whistled, his pleasure in the chocolate biscuits Steffi arranged on a plate. But it is never simple to know when these men are making a phrase or repeating it, when the words they use are words that have been used before or made up for the moment; she asked Gustave, and he said, it's a line from Pound, not a penny's worth or groat's worth or goat's worth or wordsworth or goldsmith—he likes to make bad jokes *auf Englisch*—but Pound. The Rabbi Ben Ezra himself. What thou lovest well remains.

Except there is so little left, so little that she lovest well: the scent of rosewater perhaps. A bar of Yardley soap. The way Emmanuel Feuermann manipulated the cello, and how his fingers flew across the fingerboard with such articulate precision, the *glissandi* and the *pizzicati* as separate each from the other as the desert from the sea. His widow Eva comes to visit, bringing seedless grapes, and they sit together often, regarding each other, regarding the wall. To have been born before the motorcar, to have been young in the electric age and watch the lights go on in town and illumination in the streets and houses everywhere and then the lights go out again because of the Luftwaffe—airplanes and bombs and the ensuing man-delivered darkness—to have lived as long as she has, she tells her visitors, is to have lived enough. *Das ist genug, Uncle Max.* In Hamburg once her Karlchen had a birthday party, and the cook prepared a cake for him with his favorite whipped cream, but when the bowl was passed from guest to guest at table Uncle Max helped himself twice, liberally, heaping the cream, until little Karl could take it no longer, fearing there'd be nothing left, and he cried out so everyone heard him, It is enough, Uncle Max.

This is a family joke. There had always been cream in abundance, always a sufficiency to serve with cake, and more than enough made by Hannah in the kitchen to go around the table twice. Yet Elsa remembers inflation, the wild rise of the Deutschemark when nothing was ever sufficient. One day you think you can afford what the next day proves impossible; one day a thousand marks mean something actual, consequential, and the next day they require three thousand and the next afternoon ten. Money had no meaning then; it was only what you could barter that mattered, only the form of exchange. In the worst of the inflation, *zum Beispiel,* the family airedale killed a chicken, a laying chicken in the garden of the Batschelders next door, and although she needed to do nothing about it since the act was a function of instinct not guilt, the behavior of a dog unleashed, she was a responsible neighbor and therefore she offered to pay.

She sent Karl across the garden wall to inquire how much money the dead animal would cost, and the sum was enormous, in millions, but everyone had millions then and Elsa had agreed. Therefore her son loaded a wheelbarrow with the inflated paper currency and took it to the neighbors, but in the ten minutes it took while he made the delivery the price of a chicken increased.

Because, said Frau Batschelder over the wall, you must also consider the loss of the eggs we would have had for breakfast. It is not only the chicken, she said, but also our *frühstuck* for weeks.

But at a certain point enough must be enough. This is as true for whipped cream as for Deutschemark in payment for a chicken, and certainly true of old age; she will live to be nearly one hundred and at the table where they serve the cake she wants to cry *Genug*. In her ninety-seventh year she cries out *Genug* and raises her hand to the maid. The pert impertinent young thing—another of those *au pair* girls Steffi acquires and changes each summer, a girl from Bonn or Bern or Basel or Berlin, she never can remember, and this is merely the cities commencing with "B"—will take away her cigarettes, not by mistake but intention, until she, Elsa, raises her cane. She barely strikes the maid, just once about the shoulders and perhaps also once on the ear but the girl stumbles and falls down the stairs.

Then there's a hullaballoo. The girl is weeping, and her shirt is torn, and she lies there with her arm over her face and much of her breast on display. For her own part *selbstverständlich* it is sweet revenge; she has struck a blow for dignity and privacy and stands on the landing and smiles. *Bist du verrückt, Mama,* Gustave asks her, have you gone wholly insane? Elsa will not deign to answer; instead she stands there waiting, smiling, standing on the landing. *Wilkommen, wilkommen, süsser Bräutigam,* she says, welcome, my sweet bridegroom death.

Book
Two

I

Gustave: 1946

RETURNING FROM THE GALLERY, Gustave walks through the warren of streets to Green Park, then takes the underground to Leicester Square and changes for the Northern Line to Hampstead where he lives. The trip takes fifty minutes at most. According to his mood or if Steffi has called to remind him to collect the cleaning or a piece of fish from Thompson's or just for the sake of variety—something nags at him this evening, though he cannot quite define it—he gets off the tube at Belsize Park or the next station, Hampstead itself. His home lies equidistant from each.

This day the late spring air is mild, with a rinsed aftermath of rain, and therefore he elects the second stop, the center of the village, and strolls past light-filled windows or already shuttered shops. Near the entrance to the lift a man is whistling tunelessly, and somehow the notes of his nonsense song resolve themselves in Gustave's head into

Die schöne Müllerin, and the melody stays with him where he walks. How curious, he thinks, the conversation that one carries on inside the head thus ceaselessly, the snatch of song that repeats and repeats for no discernible reason, the noise that is silence for others and, if and when we voice it, only a breach of decorum or evidenced imbalance. So each of us believes that we perform a solo when all is orchestration, *da dum, da diddledum.* Or think of Rilke's *Elegies: Wer, wenn ich schriee, hörte mich denn . . .*

Yet the lines of the elegy have modulated also, and from *Who, if I cried, would listen to me then . . .* he returns to *da dum, dadiddlededum.*

"Evenin', guv'," he hears, but he is not the one the speaker speaks to.

"Good evening," comes the answer from his left.

On the hill the rain is mizzling and the fog a porous entity through which he moves as though it were liquid made dimensional, wetly particulate, a curtain to part that stays nonetheless sealed. Somewhere a bell sounds; then engines, a horn. The pleasant rush and bustle of a day drawn down and fading towards its dark lambent completion, the women with their string bags and ankle-length raincoats unbuttoned, the children skipping down the street and old men toiling up it—all these signal safety to Gustave, an earned and poised civility, and he is in no rush. His mother and his wife and daughter and his mother-in-law and the maid are gathered together in Lyndhurst Road, the three generations awaiting their meal, the five of them engaged in constant disputation, and between the noise of commerce and the day's work at the gallery, between what he

has left behind and what he goes to for the night he rel-
ishes this interval, a brief space of solitude, walking.

He consults his watch: 6:42. What, he wonders, is the
source of his disquiet, what has he forgotten to remember
and is there an errand he has to perform: the tailor's, the
stationer's, vintner's—what was he supposed to collect? He
thinks he might telephone Steffi to ask, since the booth on
the corner stands vacant, and he could enter and inquire:
what have I forgotten, what else did we want?

A taxi appears, disappears. A newspaper vendor bran-
dishes the evening's wares, shouting, "Rail strike possible!"; a man stops to purchase a paper, and the vendor
tips his cap. Two shop girls stand at the door of the confectioner's, their hands on their hips, peering out; there are
coffee cakes and tarts and lemon cakes and *mille-feuilles*
and chocolate-dipped strawberries in the window: the new-
found abundance of peacetime.

Gustave lingers for an instant, regarding the display. The
window has a lit lamp in it, and there are biscuits and
buns. This commercial cornucopia remains only half-filled
at present, however—suggestive of a promised plenitude
but still constrained by rationing and nothing like the lush
array he remembers from the bakeries and coffeehouses
and *konditorei* of his youth. The girls' voices are high; pointing, they laugh. Involuntarily he turns his head to where
they look, and what they are pointing at makes him smile
also: a dalmation chasing a balloon.

At the gallery that afternoon he'd bought a Daubigny—
a small green landscape with a lake and trees darkly incised at the left edge of the composition. There is a
shepherd in the middle distance and several grazing sheep.
The seller, Phillip Hayes, had been more than usually
furtive, carrying the picture in his passe-partout as though
it had been contraband, wrapping the whole in brown
paper and insisting on their privacy in the partners' office.
He had not shaved; his clothes reeked. His eyes rolled; he
jabbed at the frame. With a flourish, as though extracting
a rabbit from a top hat, he shook the picture free.

Such behavior was, however, habitual with Hayes—the
younger son of a wealthy solicitor from, if Gustave remembers correctly, Lincoln or some other provincial out-
post like Manchester or York—and only remarkable in the
degree to which he paced, gesticulating, saying, "G., you
can see for yourself it's the genuine article, it's one of the
best things that Daubigny's done."

He could not disagree. The color was luminous and the
composition engagingly off center, and the price that Hayes
demanded—he was selling off his inheritance, picture by
picture—not wrong. For form's sake he haggled, since
Hayes expected it of him, and they reduced the cost by
fifty guineas and Gustave wrote out a cheque. As always,
he permitted himself a small inward flare of pleasure, an
instant of self-congratulation: well done. He was neither
covetous nor greedy, but a new landscape or Staffordshire
figure could content him, always, as though balance were
restored again and what was lost was found. In a world
adrift as ours, so full of willed barbarity, it is important

that a picture with a shepherd be acquired and a claim be lodged for lastingness: *wohlgetan*, well done.

Therefore, again for form's sake, he broke out the sherry, and his visitor drank off his glass in a gulp. "Well," said Hayes, "you've robbed me again," and went away cheerfully, weaving.

While this transpired in the downstairs office, he could hear activity in the public rooms. The doorbell chimed; what sounded like a wheelchair rolled and bumped above his head on the parquet. "You must give my best to the family," he distinctly heard a woman say, and someone else called, "Ta-ta." On the first floor of the gallery Lillian Burleigh was showing Forain: a series of sketches of lawyers she'd bought in job lots last autumn. By the end of the afternoon two had been sold: a lawyer in a flowing robe gesticulating at the bench, another in his chambers drinking wine. The graphics of Forain were tedious to Gustave, full of Gallic excess and colloquial exaggeration, but Lillian claimed he out-Daumiered Daumier.

The three partners had an agreement: if any of them wished to own an object privately they could buy out the interest of the other two at cost. He himself was collecting Rodin. Lately Lillian bought Forain and Degas, while Tolland—who was down in Fordingbridge, dealing with Augustus John—had a weak spot for examples of the female nude. This mirrored, Gustave knew, the man's personal weakness for the same subject, and the more vulgar the better; Henry was always off at lunchtime for what he called a "quick toss" in Soho and returning like a sated cat, smoothing his hair back and licking his lips. The prostitutes who worked the neighborhood of Cork Street all solicited his custom, and women in bright plumage preened near the gallery railings, asking for a cigarette or the time of day. In taxicabs and rented rooms and, once, behind a bench in Regents Park with a complaisant nursemaid, Tolland relieved himself constantly, and it was no small paradox that so knowledgeable a connoisseur and scholar of the eighteenth century should have such a taste for the gutter. The present Henry Tolland had been Heinz Teitelbaum before the war, and they had known each other since 1922, so when his old friend changed his name it was as though, Gustave liked to say, he acquired a new partner.

In the beginning the two men confined themselves to graphics, buying and selling modestly from a room off Picadilly. With the money Tolland had as an allowance from his wife and the money he himself had managed to extract from Germany, they accumulated stock: Piranesi, Tiepolo, Goya, Rembrandt and Dürer prints. It was close to the margin to start with, small beer and low percentages, but he had taken a genuine pride in making a living from what he knew best: an artist's signature. By this he did not mean, *natürlich*, the name an artist signed. It was a question of handwriting, rather, a brush stroke or a width of line, a way of bulking mass on mass or the cross-hatching on an etching, and he could recognize a signature from twenty paces off. Once you understood the fingerprint, you could not get it wrong. As a young man he had made himself an expert, preparing for the profession by long and careful study, sitting in the print rooms of the Louvre and the

Städjelik and the Pinakothek and Uffizi, and he knew what he was looking at and therefore looking for . . .

Then Lillian Burleigh joined in and the three partners bought a freehold lease on the narrow four-story brick building in Cork Street. The gallery began. Miss Burleigh was excellent with customers; she spoke uninflected English and was patently a lady and had an eye for what to hang in the public rooms. She was courteous yet definite; she knew what she wanted, and why. She had hoped to be a dancer, but her family disapproved of the stage and then she broke an ankle and turned to pictures instead.

Gustave had approached her first at the National Gallery, where she had been examining a floral arrangement by Fantin-Latour; she did so with such close attention that he could not fail to notice, and they shared a pot of tea and scones with clotted cream. She told him that she couldn't paint but did admire those who could, and she wanted to escape the tedium and predictable constraint of needlepoint and riding to hounds and a cottage in the Cotswolds with a family of children supposed to do more of the same.

"You cannot imagine," she said, "how positively stulti-fying, *stupefying* it can be to have that weight of expectation—the long, reproachful faces, the dances and the silence and the philistine conviction that whatever one would like to do just isn't done . . ."

"And what might that be?" he had asked.

"Oh, you know." She gestured expansively. "If it has some value in the world but isn't the way one's grand-mother did it, then it just isn't done."

"My own family," he said, "expected me to enter the family business. But anyhow I escaped it."

"How?"

"Well, Hitler helped," he said. "And I informed my parents I couldn't be in business, I would go mad at the office, and so my younger brother took a position in the firm instead."

"Was he grateful?"

"No. Well, possibly from time to time. Perhaps."

Lillian smiled. They divided the cost of the meal.

Soon enough it grew apparent that they had much in common, and by the fourth or fifth encounter he proposed that she meet Tolland also and see if she might cast her lot—it was the way he put it—with "two refugees." That meeting too had gone well. They discussed their tastes in art, the way to manage and publicize a dealership, the market they did wish to enter and the market they did not. By luncheon's end, the agreement was reached and the Queen Anne building leased. There had been no romantic *frisson* or entanglement, only an equable sharing of standards and, on Miss Burleigh's part, a polite bemused indulgence of the older men. She smiled at Henry's escapades and at his own abstractedness; she called him "Gustavo," then "G.," and the contraction stuck.

～～～

The three of them commenced with Old Master paintings—an Abraham Bloemaert, an Isack Van Ostade, an Artemisia Gentileschi and a triptych attributed to a follower but in fact by Van der Weyden. To begin with there

were many pictures readily available and bargains everywhere throughout the countryside. In this regard, *natürlich*, the girl's connections helped. A second cousin would
call with a query; a school friend would want to unload
"Mummy's things" on the quiet; a great-uncle was down
on his luck. There had been a number of paintings for
which they paid laughably little, a sixpence or at most a
shilling on the pound. There had been country houses
chockablock with Defreggers and Gossaerts and family
portraits by Reynolds or Gainsborough, which the owners didn't care to keep or wish to restore or couldn't iden-
tify in the first place; you could furnish a first-rate museum
with estate sales from Surrey alone.

But it was growing harder lately; the prewar flood of
bargains was thinning to a rivulet and soon would be a
trickle. At Sotheby's and Christie's now crowds attended
auctions; Bond Street was sprouting galleries like weeds.
The marriage of art and commerce is not always wholly
happy, and the art world has a clientele with peculiar tastes
in art. Very few know what to look for, and most are shockingly ignorant or at any rate parochial; they require horses
not cows in the scene or want only haystacks not cliffs.
They want something for the blue room or something to
go with the green . . .

Here the female touch proved useful; here too Miss
Burleigh's training served them well. In order to encour-
age buyers for those pictures that they hoped to sell, she
placed red "sold" dots on the wall adjacent to those they
had borrowed and which were not for sale. She attended
to the lighting and flower arrangements and furniture. She
made slipcovers for the chairs and rotated their colors in

order to match what was hanging: brown for an exhibition of Old Master drawings, pink for a show of the Fauvists. For years she tried to teach him etiquette in the English fashion, but he proved inattentive and she did not succeed.

At first he made customers welcome, saying, "Good morning, madame," or "Good afternoon, sir."

Lillian corrected him, "That expression you use . . ."

"Sir?"

"Precisely."

He waited.

"It isn't correct."

"I'm sorry, I don't understand."

"It's imprecise," she explained. "You should not say 'sir' to our visitors unless they are in fact a 'sir,' in which case you must say, 'Sir Richard' or 'Sir John.'"

"I thought it was common politeness."

"Precisely. But all too common, if you understand my meaning. It suggests that you yourself are of inferior social station, and"—she gave her nervous giggle—"you are not. These things matter a good deal. For example, what's the difference between a lady who marries a title and one who has been born to it? Let's say her own given name is Jane and she marries a Lord Baltimore; would she be Lady Jane or Lady Baltimore; what form of address would it be appropriate to use?"

"I'm afraid I don't know . . ."

"Why not learn the proper usage, then?"

"Because I'm afraid I don't care . . ."

"Oh, G.," she said. "You're incorrigible. You're absolutely hopeless," and smiled and plucked lint from his sleeve.

What Remains

Stockbrokers from the City arrived with wives or what Tolland called their "companions," sleek creatures who stared at the wall. They carried muffs and handbags and umbrellas and, not infrequently, a dog. Men from the Tate or the Royal Academy would put in an appearance, as though conferring a favor and always in a rush. Over time he came to understand which customers were serious and which ones were not. Lillian warned him, however, to take no one for granted: the threadbare visitor with rotting teeth and stinking breath might be a critic or collector and that one there, the one with the frayed jacket and the buttons missing on his shirt, is in fact a duke.

The partners painted the building dark blue and hired additional staff. The mail clerk was a thief. The plumbing in the gallery broke and brown water soaked through the ceiling. It did not reach the storage room, however—thank heaven for small favors—or saturate the art. It is to be expected that the unexpected happens, and a degree of friction is, so physicists inform us, unavoidable. At times— when Tolland tried to seduce the blond receptionist, or when Lillian believed she'd fallen in love with an Italian and must make a new life in Milano—there had been a certain strain upon the collective arrangement, a hint of disagreement as to what to buy, and for how much, and when to sell, and whom to show, and even if they should continue as a team.

"Sometimes I think . . ." said Lillian.

"What?"

115

She shook her head.

"Agreed," said Tolland. "Sometimes you think."

"Oh, G.," she said. "Make him behave."

"Impossible," said Gustave. "It isn't in the nature of the beast."

"The two-backed beast," responded Tolland, smirking. "The human animal."

"And what, pray, do you mean by that?"

"What distinguishes us as a species is the love of beauty, Lillian. And not the love of argument."

"Beauty?"

"Yes. That, and the oppositional thumb. Every lowly creature can engage in argument—a fight over carrion or squabble over grazing rights—but only we admire beauty . . ."

"Don't let's talk about it," said Miss Burleigh.

"No. She was enchanting, though."

"Her brother's a policeman," Gustave said.

"I said, let's not discuss it. Right?"

"All right. Just as you wish."

"I've had enough," she said. "I've had, oh, much. More than enough."

But such disagreements were rarely severe and such friction did not last. The receptionist moved to the Redfern next door; the Italian turned out to be married already and was of course a Catholic and unable to divorce. Although Miss Burleigh aged gracefully, it grew clear that she was aging, and her dancer's darting litheness slowed to a stately walk. Gustave produced a daughter and Tolland had a son. Both of the men sent flowers when Lillian fetched up in the hospital with what was to prove her annual siege of *petit mal* and then *tic douleureux.* She took up gardening with an apologetic vengeance, saying, "It's predictable, I know it's shockingly predictable, but I do like to watch things grow and do seem to have a green thumb."

The partners shared tea every morning and discussed the day's arrangements: who would travel, who would mind the shop and, at the auctions, how high to bid. By now they had established a routine. They took their holidays in sequence and took primary responsibility, turn by turn, for what would be hung in the four public rooms. They planned one-man shows of Roderic O'Conor and Walter Sickert; they mounted exhibitions with themes such as "Landscape" or "The Self-Portrait" or "Cezanne and his Circle at Aix." They showed Ben Nicholson and Max Ernst and Josef Herman but drew the line at abstraction; other galleries could jump on that ill-made and overpraised bandwagon, as Gustave said, but he himself would not ride it; he himself preferred to walk.

With the arrival of peacetime and the surge in tourist traffic—Americans with bulging wallets flocked to the Burlington Arcade and Savile Row around the corner— the profits of the gallery increased. This afternoon had been no exception: one purchase, two sales, each of them advantageous and he could not complain.

~⸎~

Nor would it help in any case; complaint is irrelevant here. He consults his watch: 6:54. Mildly, unimportantly, the rain begins to fall once more; mist burnishes the pavement and thickens the light of the lamps. An elderly woman approaches, a red umbrella in her hand, a toy poodle straining behind her, and Gustave raises his hat. She smiles. *Ein jeder Engel ist schrecklich.* The poodle wags its tail and squats, relieving itself. English has no translation for *schrecklich,* he thinks—*Each single angel is* . . . what: *terrible, awesome, horrible, fierce?*—and that is just as well.

When he himself was young he failed to notice the gathering storm and how it grew and darkened, but had thought all things would be—what is the expression *auf Englisch?*— cakes and ale. He went dancing and was flirtatious and had had—what would you call them?—admirers, and some he admired in turn. He had expected parties, and afterwards a driver, or if he chose to walk instead the rain-slick paving and the welcoming green grass. When we are young we think we are exempt from harm, and this can be a saving grace but more often the reverse; more often what we do so thoughtlessly we think about long afterwards and, thinking of it, feel regret.

What, he wonders, if he himself had stayed in Hamburg, in his father's business, or if Hitler had not come to power or the Weimar Republic dissolved? What if he had not married Steffi or become a dealer with a gallery on Cork Street? What if he had no daughter or instead had had a son? What *might have been* defies all fruitful contemplation, since the world is everything that is the case and only and completely what it is . . .

The human animal is, however, full of expectation: anticipatory pleasure or after-the-fact regret. One of the curiosities of the species, Gustave tells himself—arrested by a chiffon hat and red silk gown in the window of Milady's

Milliner—is how we live so much in the conditional, the "might-have-been" or "what if." That great Kantean *als ob* has bedeviled the century, he believes, and he no more imagines what it would be like to ask that pair of shop girls from the bakery to model such chinoiserie or share a pint at the King's Arms than he imagines what it would be like to huddle shivering by the paraffin stove in Phillip Hayes's laudanum fit. Henry Tolland would have certainly imagined it and acted on the fancy; he would have accosted both the girls and in the morning offer a remark about confectioner's sugar and bringing sweets to the sweet.

But he himself has no such need; he is satisfied to walk these wet streets in the enveloping dark. Well, not satisfied exactly, he admits to the pavement, not content. But what is the source of his failed satisfaction; which is the sorrow that shadows him home? *Und gesetzt selbst, es nähme einer mich plötzlich ans Herz: ich verginge von seinem stärkeren Dasein.* In the near distance above King's Row, muffled, churchbells chime. *And even if an angel pressed me suddenly against his heart I would collapse in its stronger existence* . . .

Wind carries the smell of fried fish. He sets no stock by birthdays but in December will turn forty-three. He has his health, *Gott sei dank.* His teeth bother him a little and his hair is turning white, but he wakes up in the morning without any pain or stiffness and all of his bodily functions work well; Dr. Lucas pronounced him as sound as a penny but said he might lose an occasional pound. From such a fat man as Dr. Lucas, this advice seems peculiar in the extreme and perhaps intended as a witticism: *penny, pound.*

But Lucas has never been known for his humor, and Gustave resolves to abjure Steffi's sweets; she makes an excellent *Baumkuche,* and also a raspberry compote of which he is fond. On holiday this year in Switzerland they will traverse the Allaline Glacier, and that should be invigorating, and perhaps this weekend also he will take Mama to Bournemouth so that she might see the sea. Above the streetlamp up the hill the moon emerges hazily, a day or two until the full, and he reminds himself what pleasure it would give his mother to walk along the beach and breathe in salt sea air . . .

Seven o'clock. The rain has stopped. He turns left at the crescent and climbs his own hill. On Eldon Grove a couple stands embracing in a doorway, and he wonders if they understand or care that they are being watched. The girl has her skirt rucked up over her knees, its fabric pulled taut by the arms of her swain, and Gustave finds this sight disquieting; how quickly one leaves Rilke, Wittgenstein and Kant for a chance view of distant flesh; how curious—and he pauses an instant, bemused: how *mortifying* that a man should be thus mortified—to lose one's train of thought because of three inches of leg. *Da dum, da dumdededum.*

In the house in Hampstead things continue as before. His mother and mother-in-law are at each other's throats, as usual, and Steffi occupies herself with charity cases in Golders Green. The Swiss *au pair* girl, AnnaLise, will have to be replaced. She comes from a suburb of Basel and is planning to return in June; she has three sisters and four brothers and had wanted to improve her English in order to become an English teacher at home. Yesterday while he was filling the paraffin stoves AnnaLise inquired, "Do you know Basel?" and Gustave said, "Not well." Then he made a joke about the brown bears in the entrance garden, and how it wasn't easy therefore to enjoy an evening's stroll, and she said, "You are speaking of Bern."

"Are they in the same canton?" he asked, using the word, pleased with himself for knowing that Switzerland consisted of twenty-two cantons, and she told him, "No."

"Do you speak *Schweitzerdeutsch*?" he asked, and she said, "Of course I do, yes."

AnnaLise was blond and plump and plain. They shared a glass of cider in the kitchen, and he could think of nothing else to say and, leaving, asked, "Do you have friends? Or have you been lonely here?"

"I haff no friends," she said, and what appeared to be moisture gathered in her eyes.

His brother and his brother's wife and their two sons will go. They are sailing for America next week. Now he reaches his own home's front garden—the roof slates darkly gleaming, the light on in the drawing room—and opens his own wooden gate. He will miss them very much. Gustave is not demonstrative or given to such speeches, but he feels as though he could in fact deliver such a speech; it is this which had been troubling him all day.

He puts his finger on it finally—the vague disquiet, the sense that those who thronged the gallery were intruding on his privacy, the irritation with the young couple just now on Eldon Grove. It is not the evening's hint of heat, not his premonitory weariness with the scene to come at table, not the shop girls' shrill vulgarity or the mizzling damp. *Wer, wenn ich schriee, hörte mich denn aus der Engel ord-*

nungen? His brother and his brother's family are leaving. *Who, if I cried, would listen to me then from the Angelic orders?* There has been privation sufficient; there have been departures enough.

II

Jacob: 1946

On the boat his baby brother gets long pants. The voyage takes eleven days; on the sixth day, which is more than half and closer to America, Ben gets a pair of flannels like the pair that Jacob has. They are dark gray with pleats and cuffs, because boys in America wear long pants but boys in England who are four years old do not. He himself has worn long pants for two whole years already but his brother only wears them in the dining room at night. Because Ben can't wear them all the time, their mother says, because he mustn't spoil them and must look presentable when he gets off on the other side and meets their Omi and Opi and also Uncle Fritz. It will take eleven days on the westward crossing, but before that it took months. And the *Queen Mary* and the *Queen Elizabeth* can make the trip, their father says, full speed ahead in five. Before the invention of steam there were sails, and when you took a sailing ship it took a long long time. Because now we have an engine and before they had only the wind.

It was Mummy who got seasick, who feels *übel* every day. Sometimes she feels better and sometimes she is Bessie I'm a little messy, but always she feels *übel* and sits on a chair on the deck. There are twenty people on this ship if you don't count the sailors and the captain and the cook and what they call the stewards and the first and second mates; there are twenty passengers traveling across the wide Atlantic Ocean all the way to Tampa, Florida, and then there'll be a train. Down in the hold they hold crates. You can tell the way the wind blows by the way the smoke travels, says their father, and what we leave behind us is called wake.

At the dock in Liverpool they got all aboard by a gangway which isn't a gangplank to walk. You walk up it holding carefully, carefully onto the rail but when you walk the gangplank if the ship's a pirate ship instead you jump. They have two rooms on the freighter which is called the *Nellie* and the steward says *Old Nell.* He did feel seasick on the second day but not so very much because it doesn't matter, Daddy says, and last year he had the whooping cough which made him feel much worse. When he had the whooping cough it made him feel much worse than this, and he tells his baby brother well let's go up on deck. Do you remember Dr. Samson said my whooping cough was very bad but not so bad it meant the hospital, and you had to sleep in Mummy's room and couldn't stay in ours?

They play checkers and watch seagulls on what is called the updraft, where they float and jerk their heads but barely, and barely move their wings. Gulls eat what the passengers throw. They dive and eat the wake. In the Irish Sea it was busy and exciting for Britannia rules the waves, and always has, and *hoffentlich* still will, their father says; on the first night of the voyage out, Jacob lay in what they called his berth but not the kind of birth where you are born, where they bring jam, and the rocking is just like a cradle, he told his baby brother, not a problem, and the next day there was sunshine on the green and white-topped waves; it is sea spume, it is *Meerschaum*, Mummy tells them, foam and spray. What Daddy uses to sketch with is charcoal, and also a good red pencil and also when he has the time a watercolor box. I have always loved to paint, he says, and sometimes I believe I could have been a painter, but of course there is the business and our family to feed. Of course there was the war.

The steward is called Jimmy and the first mate's name is Jim and the cabin boy is Bob; where they come from is Liverpool and Manchester and Newcastle-on-Tyne. They were proper English navvies once but now they man this ship. At the table in the dining room the family must sit with Madame Huizinga and Mr. and Mrs. Pincus, but he tucks in his napkin between his collar and his chin and rubs Jacob's cheek, saying how well the boy has shaved today and winking and saying my boy why don't you call me Pink. Then he says might I have the dish of butter there, might I trouble you for salt. He and Mummy talk together, they have many things in common, and when she isn't feeling *übel* they sit on the deck and play chess. It's a great piece of good luck, says their new friend Mr. Pincus, that we should share a table on this trip.

"What were you doing in England?" their father asks.

"Visiting," says Mrs. Pink.

They are sitting at the table and waiting for dessert. The food is bad, says Pink, but at least there isn't much of it. He laughs.

"Do you go there often?" Mummy asks.

"Where?"

"Europe." This is called, she tells the children, making conversation; this is how to be polite. They can only be excused if they ask to be excused.

"We hadn't ever been before," says Mrs. Pink. Her hair is red. "But now the war is over, so I said, 'Pink, let's us be tourists. Let's go see Big Ben and the Tower of London, Windsor Castle. Everything.' And he said, 'Surely, Mrs. Pink'—it's what he calls me, 'Mrs. Pink'—'if that's what you want for our wedding anniversary, then it's just what you're going to get.'" She smiles at Jacob. "It's a beautiful country, your England," she says. "So green, with wonderful gardens."

"What did you like best?" asks Madame Huizinga. "Which part of England did you prefer?" She uses smelling salts. She wipes her lip.

"Oh, everything," says Mrs. Pink. "I liked to listen to Big Ben, the clock you're named for," she turns towards Ben, "and look at Parliament. Windsor Castle. The Changing of the Guard at Buckingham Palace, naturally, and the Tower of London with those big old, those old, those what do you call them . . . ?"

"Turrets," says Pink.

She shakes her head. She wears a hat.

"Battlements? Escarpments?"

"Dungeons," Jacob says.

Their father has taken out his sketchbook and is sketching Mrs. Pink. "With your permission," he says. But he makes her nose too big. She smiles at him and he smiles back and says, "Just a minute, just a minute," and draws her earrings on her ears and also the necklace she wears.

"You must come and see us in Georgia," says Pink. "Julia. Karl. You'll like it," he says to the boys.

They nod.

"Try to imagine," says Pink, "that people made this crossing often many years ago. Before there were steam engines, when the only thing that got them to the other side was wind. And the tides and the currents, of course." He finishes his glass of wine. "When they were trading for a product called sea-island long-staple cotton. Or for tobacco, maybe, they'd fill the hold of clipper ships with cobblestones. To give a ship weight for the journey, you see, to act as ballast for the trip and then they'd dump cobblestones out in the harbor and load back up again. And that's why Savannah has cobbles."

"What's cobbles?" Jacob asks.

"You'll see, my boy. Next week."

"But there were slave ships also," Mrs. Pink reminds her husband. "You shouldn't be ignoring that. You shouldn't make it sound like everything was wonderful."

"No."

"That Ruy López opening," says Mummy. "The one you used this morning. It rarely works."

"*Jiocco piano,*" Pink announces to the table. "It's what I prefer."

Madame Huizinga departs; she folds up her napkin and stands. "Good people, I must take my leave. I'll see you all this evening, will I not."

Pink and their father stand. These are manners; these are good manners; this is the way to behave. "Will I not," Pink repeats.

His family has been in Georgia since before the war. What war is that? their father asks, and he says the Civil War, the War between the States. I didn't know that Jews were in the South that long ago, their father says, and Pink says *au contraire.* There were peddlers everywhere, and also dry-goods stores and banks; my great-grandfather, he says, went to Atlanta in the 1830s, and we never left. Well, during the war for a time. The Civil War, you understand, which in Atlanta they still call the late unpleasantness. When General Sherman marched on through and said war is, well, heck. I didn't want to tell your boys about the middle passage; why talk about the trade in slaves, do you think that I did the right thing?

Then the waiter with the crumber comes and scrapes the mess that Benjamin made, and then he scrapes where Jacob ate so everything is clean again. Then Mrs. Pink and Mummy say let's take a turn about the deck, and Daddy closes his sketchpad and says How about a game of shuffleboard, *Kinder,* my boys?

Up on deck the sun is shining and the place where they play shuffleboard is portside which means left. But there are other people playing and so they have to wait. Ten minutes only, says their father, and then he takes his pencil out and begins another sketch; to starboard means the right. Their mother leans over the rail. She has her eyes narrowed, but watching, and she pats the post beside her and Jacob comes and watches by her side. If he puts his head between the ropes he can lean over the rope, not the rail, and she tells him to be careful and he says she mustn't worry he did it this morning by himself, and she takes his hand. Oh, do be careful, Jacob, please. Do you know what we are looking at? she asks.

He remembers Granny telling him to look at things, not name them, and he answers blue.

Then she says not exactly, and he tells her green.

But Mummy has a different answer and a way of looking which is, she says, a way that's different than Granny's or your father's; do you see this? It is metal painted white and blue, and the object by that object is round and white with ropes. Except each of them have names.

These are what we call bulkheads and stanchions, she says, and the world is a storehouse of language; when I say steamship, for example, I mean something very different than a clipper ship or tug; there are words for everything, my darling, and the more of them you know the more you'll understand and then the more clearly you'll see.

I myself, she says, had never heard the words bulkhead or stanchion before this trip, but now I have acquired them and possess a new understanding and an additional important piece of information in my mind. The world exists in language, according to certain philosophers, and though I do not entirely agree with them they are not entirely wrong. Here are lifeboats, for example, and here are life preservers and it helps to know their names. So if I hear a stranger talk about bulkheads and stanchions and clipper ships, or if someone says we must assemble by the lifeboats and check your life preserver I know just what he means.

You try, she says, and Jacob shuts his eyes and sees them: *stanchion, bulkhead, Granny, life preserver, wind.* There are words for how I'm feeling, Mummy tells him, and the proper word is grateful, and I want you to be grateful too for how we have been spared. Then he opens his eyes and she's crying, a little, so she blows her nose and says I'm still feeling *übel* and you mustn't pay attention and you mustn't mind. But then she says, remember, when they take away your house and kill the people that you love they can't take what you carry in your head.

Mr. and Mrs. Pincus play shuffleboard with Jacob and his brother; the brothers make a team. That's what their father says, and then he draws. The brothers get the evens, numbers two and four and six and eight, and he goes first and then Mrs. Pink goes and then Ben takes a turn and misses the ten, the silly-baby blighter, and then Pink moves it to the side and then it's Jacob's turn again and he smashes them kaboom and knocks three off the field; it's rather like cricket, he knows. The evens are red and the odd ones are black and it doesn't matter, really, but sometimes they get black. Except you do it with a stick, except the way you shuffle has to be careful because not overboard; you have to imagine, says Pink, the place you'll end up when your own turn is finished and where you want to be.

Pink's stick is a long one and his is a short; his brother gets a short stick too and Mrs. Pink a long. They play every day if the weather is fine, and this is the third time since breakfast; the game ends when the grown-ups win and Pink announces you two can't beat the odds, ha-ha, and smiles and rubs Benjamin's head. Let's have another go at it, says Jacob, we'll have revenge, we'll make you walk the plank. Well perhaps we'll take a turn again, says Mrs. Pink, later, when these other good people who've been waiting patiently have had a chance to play. Perhaps right after tea.

In the swimming pool their father swims, and he will teach Jacob to dive. Do you want to? He says yes. Are you made out of sugar? He says no. But the problem is the water moves, and the waves it makes enormously slap up against the tile; what really happens, says Daddy, is that the ship is rolling and water stays level inside. It seeks its own level, he says. This means if we roll toward starboard the water stays level at port, and the reverse is also true, do you follow, do you understand? And the water's salt water, it comes from the sea, they pipe it directly inside. If a German captain came and said halt and surrender he could swim for his life except sharks. Swimmabimma, Granny liked to say, but that was in the bathtub and then he held his nose and shut both eyes and went down underneath the water and could count to twenty and come up again. All right, says Daddy, we don't have to dive, we can go on the deck and play shuffleboard if you'd rather, and Jacob says oh please. How was it? Mummy asks him, and Daddy tells her, fine. With a little practice, he says. It isn't natural, she comforts him, it's like chess or anything worth learning; it does take patience, darling, and you'll enjoy it soon. But not till you want to, she says, not till you feel you want to learn and then she turns to her husband and says just leave the boy alone.

Jacob takes out his book. He uses Mummy's deck chair because she went below to rest and he can use her blanket on the deck. There are pictures and stories about exploration; it's a book Uncle Gustave gave him for the journey across the wide Atlantic and each page has a different ship: a frigate, a galleon, a firefighting ship, a tug, an ocean liner, a submarine, a rowboat, a tanker and a battleship called the H.M.S. *Indomitable*. When he was *übel* that first day in St. George's Channel he read the whole book twice, straight through, and learned everything about the ships and Benjamin can't read, the silly-baby blighter, just turning the pages and making it seem that he knows.

His brother has a picture book with pictures of Epaminondas, like the one about Little Black Sambo which Jacob used to read. Epaminondas carries butter for his mammy, and puts it on top of his head to keep safe, but the sun is hot and melts it and when he comes back home it looks as if his brains ran out all over his head. His mammy says, at the end of each adventure, oh Epaminondas, Epaminondas, you ain't got the sense you wuz born with. There are pictures of palm trees and alligators in the river; their father says that's what we'll see when we arrive in Florida, I wager. And the hop-skip-and-jump goes like this:

What Remains

*Eeny-meeny-miney-mo
Catch a nigger by the toe
If he hollers, let him go,
Eeny-meeny-miney-mo.*

Then the steward comes by with their afternoon tea, and there's marzipan and shortbread and a cup of broth. But she's not in her room where she said she would be when he knocks to remind her there's tea. She is not in the salon or dining room or lounge and so he goes back to the door, knocking louder, calling *Mummy,* calling *mustn't miss it,* until Pink sticks out his head from where he takes a nap across the hall and says oh Jacob, no, of course she isn't here. Now go up on the deck like a good boy, he says, and let a person rest.

—◠

"Are you happy?"
"Yes."
"Very happy?"
"Yes."
She is wearing her green dress. She is freshening her lipstick; that's what it's called, to freshen, and *zum fressen* is German instead. *Zum fressen* means to eat.
"Are you the apple of my eye?"
He nods. He turns back to the book.
"Will you promise me something, Jacob?"
"What?"
"When we get to America—the captain says tomorrow—will you remember what you see; try to remember every-

133

thing, I mean? Your first foreign country. Your first new shore."

"All right," he tells her. "Everything."

"Do you like Madame Huizinga?"

He shakes his head.

"Do you find her company pleasant?"

Again he shakes his head.

"But Pink?" she asks. "You like him, don't you?"

"Sometimes."

"Very much?"

This time he doesn't answer. He looks out the porthole instead.

"Let me explain this, darling, let me tell you so you understand. The reason you don't like her is she has no curiosity; she doesn't pay attention and she doesn't find you interesting or wish she knew us better or want to find things out."

His mother pats on powder. The powder comes after the cream.

"You know the expression," she says. "'Curiosity killed the cat.' Well that's true enough but only in a certain sense; it helps to be curious usually. But she's—there's a word for it—smug."

"Smug," Jacob repeats.

"And it's an unattractive quality, it's what growing old can do to people if they don't pay attention, correct?"

He understands, he tells her, but she repeats it anyhow: a person who gets lost in himself simply isn't a person to trust. "Your father, for example," she says, but just then his father comes into the cabin and she stands and shuts the compact case and collects her handbag and says, "Yes, well, I'm ready."

"Good evening, my son," Daddy says.

"Good evening."

"Are you ready for landing tomorrow? Packed and ready for America?"

"Remember," Mummy says. "As I always tell your father, the only reason to be married is to have children. Such children."

But before he can answer they leave.

⌒

When they come into the harbor there are freighters and steamships and tugs, and Jacob knows which one is which. A pilot comes on board to lead them to the harbor, and there are what you call bananas also, which he has seen in Ben's book. They are also in Babar, because they grow on palm trees, and King Babar and Queen Celeste enjoy them very much. They arrive on the boat with the pilot, in nets, and all the passengers get some, but Mummy says no thanks. There are green ones that are not yet ripe but the ones they give the children are yellow and so you peel them back. He gets three and Ben gets three and Mummy says you will make yourself *übel*, be careful, but it is after all fruit.

Mr. and Mrs. Pincus come across to say goodbye. "It was a pleasure meeting you," says Pink. "Julia. Karl, I hope we stay in touch." He is wearing a white hat and a bow tie and his face is red because of how much sun they've gotten up on deck. "You're looking well," says

Mummy, in that way she has when she says something that she doesn't mean, and Pink gets redder still.

Then Daddy says, "I wanted you to have this," and gives Mrs. Pink the sketch, only now her ears are pointed and her eyes in the picture stick out. He says, "It needs a proper frame."

"I'll put it in our living room," says Mrs. Pink. "It will remind me."

"Of what?" Mummy asks. "Ships passing in the night?"

"It was a pleasure beating you at shuffleboard," says Pink, but Jacob doesn't laugh.

Mummy shakes her partner's hand. "A pleasure playing chess," she says.

"Yes," says Mr. Pink.

"*J'adoube*," their mother says.

They stand there all together, and Jacob eats bananas and says Ben never had a banana before.

"Why don't you come visit Atlanta?" asks Mrs. Pink. "Come see us there."

They are standing on the deck. Birds wheel and shriek above their heads, and there's what you call a pelican and also a flamingo, which is what Jimmy the steward calls them; he has fetched up the family's luggage and he deserves a tip. When somebody performs a service, when they make the journey pleasant for you, then you tip them, Daddy says, that's what a gentleman does. You must always live beyond your means, and one of the best ways to do that is by generosity to those who are less fortunate.

Their father gives Jimmy five pounds.

"I'm much obliged, sir," Jimmy says. He touches the braid on his cap. The sailors throw down rope and some-

where below men throw ropes back, and the steam w
tle blows, and the foghorn, and there is what you ca.
commotion, a hullabaloo. "What's *j'adoube*?" he wants
know, and his father says, "It's a term in chess, it mear
touch a piece but not move it, it means make adjustment.
in French."

Madame Huizinga sits in a deck chair, her suitcase beside her, her steamer trunks at the ready, and they take
out their passports, and the customs men arrive. Madame
Huizinga wears a gray hat. They must make an inspec-
tion, Daddy says, to make certain the things that we bring
to America are things that America will accept; what about
you, *Kinder*, do you have your suitcases packed?

Jacob tells him yes we do, I helped him with his suitcase strap, and Ben says no he didn't I can do it by myself. Then they go to the rail and look down. The men
on the dock look all wrong. They are called stevedores,
he knows, and wear long blue pants and red handker-
chiefs and many of them are half-naked and Jacob sees
their muscles moving and their white teeth when they
shout. They are wearing paint, he thinks, or funny shirts
for the sun. But their skin is burnt, is brown and black,
and suddenly he knows he's looking at Epaminondas or
Little Black Sambo, but grown up, and turns to his parents and says Mummy, look, there's *niggers*, and she slaps
him, hard.

He says niggers again and she says don't ever use that
word, and then the bananas come rushing back up and
he vomits all over his pants. The custom man says welcome to Tampa and chalks an X on his suitcase, and
Madame Huizinga pulls out her smelling salts and hand-

kerchief. You silly-billy, Benjamin says, you ruddy smelly blighter, and Jacob cries and tells them rubbish rubbish rubbish I don't ever want to be here I only want to go home.

III

~~~~~~

1946

THEY RETURN TO ENGLAND on the H.M.S. *Queen Mary*
of the Cunard Line. "It is enormous," says Jacob, and he
knows other words for enormous and lists them: "It is
tremendous. Huge, vast." The crossing takes five days.
"The summer is over, the journey is ending, the wind is at
our backs." That is the poem his little brother makes a
rhyme for, a stupid poem, Jacob tells him: *cover, sending,
sacks*.

"Why is it so stupid, what's so stupid?" Benjamin keeps
asking.

"Mind your own beeswax," he says.

But what Jacob remembers to start with is the taxi at
the dock, the policemen and the cabbies and the porters
and the crowd, the soldiers still in uniform and women
with babies and dogs. The noise became corporeal, a pool
of sound loudly accreting, a clattering chatter through
which he must move, a concatenation of machinery and

139

whistles and the fuss and ruckus of farewell. There are luggage wagons everywhere, a gangway festooned with red ribbon, and he and his brother both wear Yankee baseball caps. They arrive at three o'clock while everyone can come on board; departure is scheduled for six. His grandparents Omi and Opi appear, and Aunt Ilse who will drive them home again, and Uncle Fritz sends flowers but could not manage, unfortunately, to be free this afternoon himself. His telegram read *Bon Voyage und Wiedersehen and Love.*

They have sojourned in New York. This is the word Julia uses, for we have been, she likes to say, wayfarers and sojourners and not tourists in New York. Nonetheless they did what tourists do; they traversed the Hudson and East Rivers and circled the Statue of Liberty and visited the zoo and next day the top of the Empire State. This impresses the children considerably; they take the elevator and lean out and see, or so they declare to each other, everything for miles. If you drop a penny from the top of the Empire State, Jacob knows, the person underneath you will be killed; the penny would go right through their heads and through their feet and three feet down into the pavement if they happen to be standing there. He tells his little brother it's the tallest building in the world, not like the side of a mountain but straight up. Not to mention what would happen if you jumped.

"Well in that case let's not mention it," says Karl.

"I was only explaining," says Jacob.

His father says, "Well, don't."

"I was only telling Ben," he says.

"Genug."

This means their father means it, so the brothers pro-

ceed to the window in the observation deck, and Jacob
points out where New Jersey is and which one is the
Chrysler Building, the second tallest structure in Manhattan and therefore the whole world.

"I will miss you, *Liebchen*," Omi says.

"Yes."

"I enjoyed our visit very much."

"We both did," Opi says. "You must come see us in the
future soon again. Hurry back."

"When we can," Julia promises her parents. "As soon
as ever possible. We are discussing it."

"*Gewiss*," says the grandmother. "Certainly. It was very
pleasant, darling, to have been a family once more."

She wears pink and lavender clothing, not only black
and gray; she keeps an appointment with the hairdresser
weekly and in addition has a manicure and pedicure and
must keep up appearances because a woman should not
let herself go and take such things for granted. Omi carries an alligator handbag with gold clasps and, because it
is summer, her parasol and raincoat but not fur. Also, Julia
tells her sons there is truth in the old saying that clothes
do make the man. Papa's cigars are of the very finest tobacco, you can tell this by the length of ash; he acquired
them in Cuba when they escaped to Cuba, and also he
wears hand-stitched shoes. "My father himself is a dandy,
you see, a regular Beau Brummel as far as his clothes are
concerned.

"His suits are smart," she continues, "you can tell it by
the quality in such a thing as buttonholes. Notice the way
the tailor sewed them and you can tell immediately this
suit has been hand-cut. We are not rich enough," she says,

"to buy anything except the best, because the very best is economical; it lasts. And so when you see that a person has paid attention to such details then you know the person is attentive; a gentleman or lady pays attention, always, and would not go out in public with, for example, holes in her pockets or an open handbag or cigarette ash on a skirt."

Jacob knows about the *Lusitania* and the way it sank. He knows about the famous *Titanic* and what happened to it years ago, how it had been unsinkable but sank. There was an iceberg, he tells Benjamin, and a captain who cried, "Full speed ahead, damn the torpedoes," and then it hit the iceberg and the great brave ship went down. The *Queen Mary* was a troop ship in the war, and so the decks and the funnels were painted not black and red but blue and brown and green; that way the German airplanes and the zeppelins don't notice, he tells his brother, which is called camouflage.

"Well, what about the submarines?" asks Ben.

"They would look up, not down, of course. So I suppose," says Jacob, "they must have painted the bottom of the ship light green, which is the color that a submarine would see if it was diving underneath and looking up through what you call a periscope." "Do you think so?" Ben asks their father, and Karl tells them, "Possibly. Quite possibly. *Veilleicht.*"

"The *Titanic* was unsinkable," says Jacob, "but anyhow it sank. What would you do if it sank? Let's say you were a battleship like the S.S. *Ironsides* and thought you were invincible, which means you can't be beaten, but suddenly this wall of ice comes at you in the fog and mist, the *Nacht und Nebel,* careful, *Vorsicht!* and everyone is playing music, 'Nearer My God to Thee,' let's say you take the women and the children first and put them in the lifeboats, which is the way it goes, and suddenly this German U-boat comes along and says, the captain standing up on deck and using a bullhorn, '*Surrender,*' well, what would you do then?"

"I would row for my life," Ben answers.

And Jacob says, "Not enough oars."

"I would jump overboard and swim for my life."

"But you couldn't do it fast enough, and anyhow there's sharks."

In their stateroom they have everything they could possibly need, their father says, for a journey such as this one; they have a basin and a closet and the steward takes the beds down and plumps the pillows, expertly smoothing the blankets, and the children watch him work the porthole and rearrange the room. In First Class the beds are larger, and the appointments are, says their mother, much more suitable, but they couldn't get a booking and this will have to do. Besides, says their father, frowning, do you think I'm made of money? and Julia says I used to think so, yes.

Out the porthole the children see sea. There is brass that's brightly polished and wood that's well oiled, gleaming, and then Karl teaches them the song about the admiral who polished up the handle on the big brass door. In the H.M.S. *Pinafore,* he tells them, there's a chorus they must learn to sing: "Well, he *polished* up the handle so carefully that now he is the ruler of the *Queen's Navy.*"

In the ship's newspaper they read that the Right Honorable Harold Witt is traveling First Class, and Karl wonders if that could possibly be Sir Robert Witt the solicitor's brother and if they should send him a card. According to the manifest, there's also Miss Vivien Leigh in First Class, and their mother tells the children that Miss Leigh is a beautiful actress: "Just wait till you see her, you'll see."

In the cabin their guests drink champagne. When Omi and Opi and Aunt Ilse obey the purser's announcement that all visitors must leave and only listed passengers may now remain on board, "*Last announcement, final call,*" Julia is crying a little, and she says, "I'm afraid it reminds me, I hate to say goodbye."

"But we'll meet again soon," Opi says.

"But in any case I hate it," Julia says.

⌇

"What did you like best?"

"About?"

"About America," says Mrs. Hulse. Her hair is red and curly, bobbed, and her fingernails are pink. She lives in Detroit, she tells everybody on the second evening at the table that they share; she is traveling to London since "alas, my husband is no longer with us" and his name was Patrick and he died, alas, too young. She is traveling to drown her sorrows, she explains, and what better way than to cross the wide Atlantic; have you visited Detroit?

"We were on the East Coast only," Karl replies.

"For business or pleasure?"

"Both. I myself am in the import-export business."

She turns to the boys; fidgeting, they flank her at the table. "And what did you like best about America?"

"The car," Jacob tells her.

"Car?"

"The one downstairs. The one we're taking home with us; it's down there in the hold."

She raises her eyebrows, then nods. Her lipstick is the color of her fingernails exactly. "I know nothing about automobiles," she says, as though a proper person should know nothing about automobiles and it would be a waste of time to learn. She pats her lips with her napkin and examines the shape of the mark of her mouth and folds the napkin up.

"It's a Chevrolet," Jacob explains. "A Chevy Roadster in the cargo. Black."

"How nice," she says, and signals to the waiter that she has finished her soup.

"But in Detroit," asks Karl, "doesn't everybody know all about cars?"

"Not everybody," says Mrs. Hulse. "Not every woman anyhow. I left it to Patrick entirely."

He swings his legs against his chair and Julia says, "Don't do that, Jacob," and he says, "Don't do what?"

"Not while we're eating," she says.

In America they motored on the wrong side of the road. It's the right side for America instead, the children learn, and their father sits behind the wheel on the left-hand side; he will get used to this, he promises, he will manage it in England in such a reliable car. It is large enough for everyone, much bigger than a taxi, and worse comes to worst we can sell at a profit, he says.

Why is it different in America, his brother asks, what made them make the cars that way? and Jacob says it's because it's the other side of the Atlantic Ocean and everything runs backwards, just the way that if you dug a hole, if you could manage which of course you can't, but if you could dig all the way past rock and molten fire to the other side of the world which is China then everything you looked at would be upside down.

The steamship *Queen Mary* is posh. And that word means, their father tells them, Port Out Starboard Home. It means, Karl says, you pay more money not to have the sun in your eyes in the evening, whichever way you travel, since it makes the cabin hot. And it depends also of course how high you are up in the ship, how many decks above the water or if you're situated up above the Plimsoll line. But that's another Plimsoll, he explains, not the one who lived across the street and also there are Plimsoll shoes, so when I wear my Plimsolls I am doing a different thing; this particular person by the name of Plimsoll decided how much you should put in the hold of a ship by way of ballast so the ship can continue to float. Because it means posh to be on the side where the sun doesn't heat up your cabin all day, but that's because in olden times they went around the Horn, which was from north to south. He explains this all to Jacob, drawing north and south upon the table linen with his knife, and also east and west, but I don't know the derivation of the word for snob, he says, S-N-O-B, and then Benjamin asks about China and will we stand on our heads?

Miss Vivien Leigh is posh. The boys watch her walking up and down, up and down upon the First Class deck, taking her constitutional, says Julia, because she is an actress, looking smashing by the gate that's locked. In addition there is Cabin Class, which is the one they're traveling, and Tourist Class, and Karl says there's also what people used to call steerage, which is just sleeping on the cold cold deck or all the way down in the hold. Remember Mr. Pink? he says, and the boy says yes, remember what he told us about cobbles, how in olden times the sailors would load cobblestones as cargo for the voyage out? Jacob answers yes of course and he tells his little brother how they also carried slaves from America in steerage, they just piled them up. And this was in the period when long-staple cotton was king.

"In England we have King George," says Jacob, "and there used to be King Wenceslas but in America they had King Cotton and he required slaves. And that's what the Statue of Liberty means and why she holds a torch. Because she says, 'Give me your poor, your cold, your tired and your hungry wretched masses,' and she burns up old King Cotton and will set them free; Miss Liberty undoes their fetters," Jacob says.

"What are fetters?" Ben asks.

"Oh, you know."

"I don't, and you don't either."

"Do I have to tell you everything?"

"Mind your own beeswax," Ben says.

⁓

In America the family stayed with their relatives; Uncle Fritz and his wife Ilse have settled in a small stone house in the village of Larchmont, New York. The grandparents too reside in Larchmont, on the third floor of the Stonecrest

Apartments, and it delights the boys to take the stairs and see if by running up they can meet the elevator or even perhaps get to the door of the apartment before the adults reach it. "On your mark, get set, ready, go!" Jacob shouts, and he and Benjamin race.

Omi and Opi arrived there from Cuba, to which they escaped from Berlin. Omi's cousin is Senator Lehman, who was the governor also, and that is how they got in. But Opi was a banker, Jacob knows, and he took a train to Paris and the Nazis went right through the train to take away the Jews although his papers were in order and they would have killed him if they found him but didn't find him because he knew about it already and descended at the station and bought himself a bratwurst and got on again as soon as the Nazis got off. These Nazis were the SS troops and that is very different, he tells his little brother, than the S.S. *Ironsides* or the H.M.S. *Deliverance,* which means His Majesty's Steamship, because they were looking for Opi when he wasn't on the train. It was great good fortune, Omi says, and Opi says just a matter of timing and besides I was hungry, he says.

In Larchmont they have an old poodle called Budge. "We have always had poodles," says Fritz.

"But I had an airedale in Hamburg," says Karl, "and it won second prize in a dog show, both for obedience and breeding."

"How many dogs were entered?" Fritz inquires.

Their father says, "Just two."

Then everybody laughs. Old Budge, old Budge, they call him that because he doesn't budge. In America, the children learn, there's cakes and jam enormously, and also

Lachsschinken at the delicatessan in the village, which is called Broderson's because it's owned by Mr. Broderson. "Hello, hello. What can I do for you people today?" he asks, and his sleeves are rolled up to his elbows and he wears a white bloodstained smock. "A little liverwurst," says Julia, "and also please a half pound of Genoa salami and some herring if you have it," and he says, "*Ja, gut.*"

"And perhaps a taste also of your excellent *Lachsschinken* for my father's digestion," she says.

"*Also*," says Opi, and lights his cigar. When he says *also*, Jacob learns, it doesn't mean also, it's just an expression; "*Was gibt es heute?*" what did they have in Broderson's today? *Lachsschinken* is his favorite, but it must be good Westphalian ham. He consults the watch on his gold chain, the one that he keeps in his vest pocket and holds close to his ear when it rings; he says, "Well, it's a long time since I've eaten and come along, *Kinder*, let's eat."

He himself believes in Rolex but Fritz wears a Patek Philippe. Their father has his sketchbook out and he is drawing Budge, who lies behind the sofa and is getting fat. "He doesn't get enough exercise," says Opi, "you should walk him more often, *also*, the dog. Just watch him there, dreaming of rabbits."

And then Aunt Ilse comes into the living room and says, "You may come to the table, ladies and gentlemen, lunch is ready at long last."

"Will you give me your arm?" Omi asks.

So one family lives in America and another lives in England, but they are all the same family, Jacob knows, and no one lives in Germany because the Jews have gone. Do you like it here, asks their father, *wirklich*, really and truly? And Aunt Ilse tells them it is comfortable, yes.

⁓

"Your move."

"I know."

"I'm waiting."

"I know."

"It's boring," Jacob tells his brother. "I've been waiting ten minutes already."

"I have to think."

"Don't bother. You're beaten."

"I'm not."

"You're two bishops down now already. And a pawn."

"But I have a castle," Ben says.

"So what?"

"So that means I'm going to beat you."

"Ha ha. Very funny. Your move."

"Don't rush me."

"I'm hungry," Jacob says. "There's elevenses up on the deck."

"Check."

"Check? Silly-billy, I'll take it."

"All right," Ben says. "Check again."

"You don't understand the first thing about chess. Not the first thing at all."

"Good move," says Julia, stopping by. "A very intelligent move, Ben-ben. Now you'll have mate in three."

"Not fair," the elder son complains. "Why do you always have to help?"

"He's learning," Julia says.

Mrs. Hulse does like to dance. She informs the family of the enjoyment she derives from dancing; on Wednesday evening for the final ball she will put on, she says, dancing shoes. It has been many years, she says, since she felt able to perform, but years ago—she sighs and smiles at Karl—people said I was accomplished. He stands up to pull out her chair.

"If I may have the pleasure of your company tomorrow night," she says, "I would appreciate a partner. When Patrick and I went out dancing it was certainly something to see."

Then she nods at the family, departing, and Julia tells the waiter, "Another cup of coffee, if you please."

"Why certainly, madame," he says.

While the waiter fetches coffee she says softly, "No, I will not, I assure you, make a scene. *Doch, doch,* I assure you, but what have you to say for yourself?"

"You make a mountain of a molehill, *liebchen,*" Karl says. "She has had experience in the foxtrot and the waltz, and she misses her husband and desires one last dance. It will be the final night, we can't deny her that."

"A shipboard romance," Julia says. "That's what you mean you can't deny her, am I right?"

"Not at all. Not in the slightest. She takes a great deal of pleasure, she told me, in the intricate patterns and rhythm of dance, and it would be unkind to deny her the chance to perform."

"Is that what you call a woman of pleasure?" Julia asks. "Is that how you'd describe Felicity Hulse to the boys?"

"No, no," he says. "Not really."

"Oh," she says, "really, why not?"

"Why must you make it so complicated? I only agreed to dance because she asked me, and her husband is dead now and as you know I enjoy dancing also and she has no partner."

"*Dans la présence des enfants,*" Julia says.

Jacob knows what that means now, he tells them, and so does Benjamin; they both understand the sentence. Their father says, "*Genug.* It is only politeness, the most common form of politeness, if a person asks a favor you must oblige and say yes."

"That's it," says Julia, "that's precisely the word I would also have used."

"Which word are you referring to?"

"Common. Common as dirt."

"You are making a scene," Karl says. "Need I remind you of your great friend Pink?" and then he takes a cigarette and lights it and blows out the match.

~~~

In America the family drove along the coast and up the Boston Post Road, heading north. They took the train to Norfolk, and there they purchased the black Chevrolet, then spent a week on the trip. At the end of each day's journey Karl logged how many miles they'd gone: one hundred eighty, two hundred twenty-seven, seventy-four. Jacob and Ben shared the rear seat, staring out; their parents took turns at the wheel. In America they saw the Capitol and also the White House and Lincoln Memorial and Washington Monument, but Benjamin felt *übel* and did not want to walk. In the ship's daily chronicle they report how far the ship has traveled, and there is a contest for the precise time of arrival in Southampton. "Are you happy to be going home?" inquires Mrs. Hulse the afternoon before the dance, and Jacob tells her, "Yes."

Then Julia says, "It isn't home, we're just sojourning there."

" 'Home is where the heart is,' " says Mrs. Hulse, and smiles, and shows her teeth in the American manner, and then she says, "I'll see you later, won't I, Karl?" and continues on her walk.

Jacob likes the deck chair best of all. He likes the blankets and the pillows and the biscuits and the broth and tea; he likes the marzipan and lifeboats and the life preservers marshaled by the railing; they have had lifeboat drill twice. The passengers come from their cabins and file down the hall and march up the stairs to the deck. They say, "Fancy meeting you here," laughing, jostling, standing by their boats. The sailors make everyone practice how to get into their life preservers because, says Karl, we also serve who stand and wait; then the whistle blows all clear and they march back again.

Miss Vivien Leigh arrives on the deck, and everybody cheers. "Three cheers," the children go, "Hip hip hooray," and she smiles and waves at them and Julia says, "Now there's a person everybody wants to dance with."

"*Selbstverständlich,*" Karl agrees.

In the distance Jacob sees a complicated shape, a moving cloud. It enlarges rapidly, advancing: gray then brown, then both together, dappled brown and gray. It is not an airplane or a bird or anything he's ever seen, and he asks, "Daddy, what is that?" and Ben says, "Oh, golly, what's that?"

They cluster to the lifeboat, staring where athwart the gunwale this roaring bloat object approaches. The sailors appear unconcerned. Karl shades his eyes and stares, adjusting the binoculars. "Why, that's a zeppelin," he says, "a blimp!"

"Does it belong to us?" Julia asks, sounding not cross but frightened, and he answers, "Yes, of course, it's coming out to greet us and welcome the passengers back." Felicity Hulse comes around again and jumps up and down excitedly and both the brothers jump also: home, *home*, they have come home.

IV

~~~~~

Jacob: 1948

In Holne Chase the three of them make kippers Sunday morning, when Kathleen is off for the weekend and Mummy stays upstairs asleep. Their father has bought kippers in yellow wax paper from the grocery in Golders Green, and they all like kippered herring except Mummy who hates it, she says. So the three men of the family can close the pantry door and close the doors to the kitchen and the dining room and open all the windows while fresh air comes into the kitchen and drives the smell out of the room.

Then their father lights the stove and puts the herrings in the pan and fries them till they're brown and hot, and Jacob prepares buttered toast. His brother pours the orange juice and it will be a feast, a feast, and *vorsicht*, says their father, do you need me to take out the bones? *I* don't, says Jacob, and their father says all right but, Benjamin, give me your plate. And then he takes the skin away and lifts the bone up from the middle of the kipper and says chew and swallow carefully, eat slowly, please, and do please pay attention to bones. It is best with a little lemon squeezed across to cut the salt but I myself prefer it very salty and the way the kipper tastes without any lemon at all.

They sit in front of the window and the three men in the kitchen have their secret Sunday feast. Their father says in olden days when meat or fish went rotten it was because it spoiled, and the way to keep food from spoiling was pack it in barrels of salt. Another way to manage was to hang it from a smokehouse which is why you have what's called smoked meat, but it was difficult on sailing ships to keep the smoke up all the time, which is why most fish are salted and mostly ham is smoked. There is smoked fish also, of course, and also salted beef and pork, but these are exceptions that prove the rule; I draw the line, he says, at what they call cured ham. My grandfather kept kosher and he would be shocked at this, but kippered herring is a breakfast fit for the gods. Or at least fit for three kings.

They eat. Don't smack your lips, he says, and Ben asks why not. It's not polite, he tells his baby brother, and Ben says what I'm doing here is testing for the bones. These kippers are excellent, Daddy repeats, and then he sets up the fan. Can I have another helping please? asks Jacob, and their father says there's two for each of you but Ben is feeling *übel* and doesn't want another one and doesn't even want to finish his. Why are you making that face? he asks, and his brother says the orange juice tastes bad. There are children in India starving, says Jacob, pretending to be Granny who says that sentence often — *There are children in India starving* — you must eat what's on your plate. Daddy says well Mister Blister, this is an acquired taste and not too very much to begin with is perhaps a good idea. So they eat the bitter kippers and when the three men finish they wrap them up in paper and put them in the garbage pail and take the pail outside; then they open the kitchen windows all the way out as far as they go and make the fan go as fast as it can and wash the dishes two times each and scrub the frying pan. Because the last time they ate this way their mother came into the kitchen and wrinkled her nose and said *Gott im Himmel* it stinks in here, how it stinks. And today we are determined, Daddy repeats, it will not happen again.

But it does, it happens just that way, she comes down the stairs in her nightdress and wrap and opens the door and says *phew*. Did you think I won't notice? she asks. Do you think I'm an idiot, Karl, what do you take me for? I hate the smell of kippered herrings and you cook them here on purpose to drive me straight out of the house. It isn't so terrible, *liebchen*, says Daddy, and she says oh yes it is. You have no nose, she says. For me it's the smell of the gutter, this smell of stinking fish; I am a sensitive person and have a sensitive nose. I was raised among people with standards and you are raising savages; imagine, she says, kippers, and then she runs out of the room.

~⌒

"Good *yontiff*," Dr. Lucas says.
"What does that mean? *Gut yontiff, was bedeutet das?*"

"It's a New Year's greeting," he says. "It means—"

"We don't speak Yiddish here," says Julia. "Not in this house."

"I was wishing you prosperity—"

"Well, do it in English," she says.

"Sometimes I think you are ashamed . . ."

"Ashamed of what?"

"Of being Jewish, madame. Of belonging to a family of Jews."

"Ridiculous," she says.

"Oh?"

"Of course we are Jewish. Of *course* we are Jews."

"But you don't bring them to the synagogue. Not once have I seen you in synagogue, ever. You don't keep kosher in this house, and you have a Christmas tree, even."

"It is something to celebrate," Julia says. "In Germany we had a tree."

"Well? And if I tell them good *yontiff*?"

"That doesn't mean I speak Yiddish. Or wish to."

"Forgive me," Dr. Lucas says. "*Entschuldigen Sie*, I was making a holiday wish."

"Well, don't," says Mummy. "You'll be wearing *pais* next. You'll look like a rabbi."

"The worst anti-Semites," he tells Jacob, "are the German Jews."

<hr />

Of course we must celebrate Christmas, says Daddy, and also Boxing Day. We were not born in England but we observe that holiday, says Mummy, do we not? And

so we may celebrate Father Christmas also and have a
happy Christmas and leave it to others to light a meno-
rah, and then she kisses Jacob and his baby brother and
asks which one of you this morning is the apple of my
eye? In Hamburg, Daddy says, we had a fresh-cut *Tannenbaum,* and on Christmas morning we would eat a plate
of carp.

Yes but carp are not kippers, she says. Even those who
come from Hamburg can understand the difference, can
they not? *Hummel hummel, Mors Mors,* Daddy says to Jacob,
winking, but this time Mummy does not mind because it
is a holiday and there is much to celebrate; the Marshall
plan, for instance, and what will happen soon in Palestine,
and Hans and Ilse Hesslein have had a baby girl. They
have wished for one for many years and finally a child arrived, so there is much to celebrate this year. Also, business is good.

Paul comes down from Cambridge for Christmas, and
then they bring up the goose. The butcher has prepared
it, Daddy says, but he hasn't broken the bones properly
and today the shop is closed and so we must cut through
the bones. But the knife won't work, the shears won't work,
the saw won't work, my my this goose is stubborn, Paul
declares. I tell you, I have an idea, their father says, and
they take the Christmas goose and tie it to the door of the
garage. Then they tie it to the bumper of the big black
Chevrolet and make sure the knots will hold it and then
slowly, slowly, Paul backs up the car, saying Jacob, listen
to the bones and tell me when they crack.

So he stands there while they start the car and back it,
slowly, slowly, but the rope pulls away and the whole goose

falls down. Then his father ties it up more carefully, with clever knots around its legs, and then Paul starts the car again but this time the garage door lifts and then the handle falls off. Daddy's laughing, both are laughing, and they say this is a very stubborn goose; remember in Hamburg we used to eat carp, they weren't so difficult to manage, Daddy says.

The best part of the Christmas goose is afterwards, is what you call goose-butterfat. Now the family has Gaga living in the house, whose proper name is Engel Lund and who was born in Iceland and speaks many languages and sings in them quite famously; she will give a concert soon, she hopes, in the Prince Albert Hall. She would like to sing in Covent Garden best of all, but must wait a little longer, and in the meantime she sings for the fun of it anyhow because even for a famous singer singing should be fun. And while she waits for this engagement because a person must keep busy she shows the brothers how to render fat and put it in the ice chest with the little bits of liver in, in the brown earthenware crock with the top that is cracked, and then when it gets white and soft they spread it on their toast. Or eat it with a spoon. She is jolly and wears a white apron to cook and practices her singing, always, at the stove; it is good to stand near steaming pots and kettles, Gaga says, because it clears the throat.

O Tannenbaum, o Tannenbaum
Wie schön sind Deine Blätter

Gaga sings. Her hair is white and her apron is white because everything in Iceland, she tells him, is dark all winter long. There is almost no daytime in winter, she says, and then in the summer there's almost no night. Where you are going, Gaga says, I think the climate is much better, and Jacob asks where are we going? and she says don't you know?

Our family has traveled for forever, Daddy says. He has come in the kitchen to rinse out his cup; he has been drinking tea. It's what you call the nature of Ahasuerus, and when Jacob asks him what is that he says not what but who. Ahasuerus is the name they gave in song and story to a man called the Wandering Jew. Some say we lived in Spain or Portugal a long long time ago, says Karl, and then there was the Inquisition and we had to leave. Others say we came from Hungary or possibly from Russia and the name was first Meshullam, which means moneylender. In any case our ancestors arrived in Italy, but this is before 1500 and in the cities of Padua and Venice where they established the first bank, the Banco del Giro, he says. And your great-great-great-great-grandfather's great-great-great-great-grandfather was very rich indeed. He gave three thousand ducats every year to the poor in St. Mark's Square; he was the richest Jew in Venice and some say in all Italy and was trying to buy safety for the Jews.

Gaga laughs: it didn't work. But think about three thousand ducats at five percent per annum, Daddy persists, and see how much he wasted in the effort to stay safe. Gaga bends over the steam. Sometimes the Doge was pleased and our family lived in extravagant *palazzi*; sometimes the Doge was angry and they ended up in jail. What is the Doge? asks Jacob, and his father says *Il Duce*, the Italian word for leader, or is it—he turns to Gaga, asking her—from the word for Duke? Your Latin is better than mine, Daddy says, and she says it means "to lead." Dr. Samson has come in from the living room also, and he says more or less. But we draw the line at Shylock, Daddy says.

What does that mean? Jacob asks, and he says we start with Jessica; it's in a play by Shakespeare, the one that Granny calls better in German because the Schlegel brothers were *mehr Shakespeare als Shakespeare. The Merchant of Venice*, he says. Old Shylock was a wicked man but his daughter was beautiful and generous and that's where our family started, that's the lady who began our line and whom we call our ancestor. He is joking but only half-joking; there's a grain of truth in what your father tells you, Dr. Samson says. Except that William Shakespeare did no research for his Shylock and if he did was probably thinking about someone else, the one that they accused of plotting to poison Queen Elizabeth, a physician called Roderigo Lopez who was accused and killed. It wasn't any better then for doctors than bankers, says Dr. Samson; well anyway, their father says, I take poetic license but it's in the family tree. It's the original branch.

So then we went to Vienna and to Germany and also Denmark and Sweden; for three hundred years until just recently we lived in Hamburg and were prosperous and *bürgerliche* citizens who thought we had established an enduring home. But it's just like Spain or Portugal, not to mention Hungary and Russia and everywhere else in the world; there are always inquisitions; there are always moments in our history when Jews escape or die. There are what you call ghettos for Jews, which is a word they invented in Venice; this was when our ancestors tried to buy the island of Murano, and the Doge said no. I tell you this, his father says, to tell you there's nothing special, really, in the fact of leaving; it's not a persecution but a habit, it is not that England persecutes us but we don't belong here, really, and your mother thinks America is kinder to its immigrants and therefore we should leave.

For Christmas Jacob gets soldiers and a book on King Arthur's Round Table and also a Meccano set and a pair not of mittens but of gloves. His soldiers have a private shelf, and he lines them up for battle, first the vanguard, then the serried ranks and then the commander-in-chief. This is called an exhibition, which is what Uncle Gustave does in Cork Street in the gallery, except what he shows there are paintings or sculpture, like the time he showed Rodin. Sometimes Jacob makes them face the same direction, fighting everyone against the Hun, and then he imagines the Germans have been defeated, slaughtered, their bodies piled in heaps and ready to be buried just off the edge of the shelf. But sometimes he divides them up, and they are English fighting French, and then they fight each other, *ashes, ashes, all fall down.*

He makes his exhibitions daily and as soon as he is finished Mummy comes to the bedroom to see. He tells her if the battle is Napoleon at Waterloo or Alexander the Great; he tells her if it's olden times or modern times and asks her what she thinks. Sometimes she says I'd move this here and sometimes I'd adjust that there but mostly she says excellent and very well organized, darling, and thank God it's a world now safe enough to play at war but she draws the line at German soldiers, she won't have them in the house. Is it fine to be a god of war, his father asks, or isn't it much better to be a god of peace?

~

At Lyndhurst Road the family makes music, and Gustave plays the flute. Jacob's best friend is Robert Elkeles, and he and Jacob sit and listen before they get to eat. He is leaving soon for Palestine, not Palestine but Israel when it becomes *yeretz Israel,* and they make exhibitions of soldiers together. Robert Elkeles gave him a knight on a charger with a leveled lance, because in olden times a charger was worth two yeoman even with their crossbows strung, their pikes outstretched, and so they make an exchange. He has soldiers with bucklers and halberds and shields; he has chevaliers with swords. When he makes an exhibition it is Ivanhoe against the French, or Richard Coeur de Lion. One soldier broke his leg and one of them broke off his head by falling, but there are many soldiers left and it will be a battle royal to the death.

Aunt Steffi comes from the kitchen, and Granny sits in the armchair with her copy of Boethius and cigarette and schnapps, and Lotte Pulfermacher and Edith Lowenberg arrive in time for tea. Dr. Lucas and Dr. Samson and Daddy and Gustave will finish playing soon enough, says their mother, you just have to wait a bit longer. Don't you love this second movement? Dr. Lucas asks the room, the brilliant sostenuto here, and Robert drops his head and whispers no.

They have drawn the curtains because outside it sleets. It is more *gemütlich* anyhow, says Granny, to sit inside a room where curtains have been drawn; when you are listening to music it makes it more pleasant, she says. *Ach ja*, the best way to listen to music is with your eyes closed and mouth open, since the eyes are a distraction for the ears. And for some reason the music sounds even better if you let your mouth be open also; then it enters through the pores.

But how does that keep you from falling asleep, inquires Mrs. Feingold, what's the difference in this case between listening and sleeping, if you please?

I pay attention, Granny says, and Steffi says Mama, you snore.

What makes you say so, asks Granny, and Mrs. Feingold laughs.

Please ladies, Dr. Lucas says, with your permission: *now*.

And then they start to play again and Granny shuts her eyes. Robert Elkeles is fidgeting and Ben fidgets also but Mummy says don't fidget and then Granny starts to snore. Jacob can read music and he gets to turn the pages and is standing by the piano but hearing it across the room he laughs and the other boys start laughing too till Julia says *genug*. Robert Elkeles is moving because his father is an engineer and plans to build important what you call hydraulic engines for *yeretz Israel* and so they have to move. As soon as it is Israel not Palestine, his father says, we settle there; May 14, 1948, will be a great great day. And so it is written: great day.

Let them have it, Mummy says, and Edith Lowenberg says have what? Mummy spreads her fingers, shaking them, and says the desert; they are welcome to that sand. But what about the Arabs and the camels? Edith asks, and Mummy says they can share it, there is more than enough to go around. David Ben-Gurion is a clever warrior, declares Dr. Samson, a brave and intelligent person, and if I were a little younger I would go there too. It is either America or Israel, the two promised lands, says Daddy, but I myself prefer the promise of America, the new not ancient world. And this time I promise—he smiles at his wife—on the *Queen Elizabeth* we will be traveling First Class. Robert Elkeles has Lancelot and Ivanhoe and Sir Galahad and Sir Gawain and King Arthur too. They are made out of metal and carry bright flags, the flags are metal too. But how do you know who's who at the Round Table when they're sitting, Benjamin asks, how can you tell which is the most important knight and second in importance only to the king? That's the point of the Round Table, Jacob tells his baby brother, there's someone at his right-hand side and someone at his left-hand side, but nobody sits at the bottom of the table or so far away from Arthur that they can't share the glory, and besides he wears a crown.

Our people, Dr. Lucas says, are going home again at last; there is a place where Jews belong. You could become a farmer, you could irrigate the desert and watch it grow fertile and bloom. If I forget thee, O Jerusalem, he says, and then he snaps his bow in place and closes the violin case. We will miss you, Elkeles, he finishes, but it's a great adventure, and Mummy says castles in sand.

~~~~~~

Their father's office is in Leadenhall Street, which is the City of London. Mr. Sterner works in Kentish Town, which is where they keep the warehouse, but Johnny Weiser works in the office, and so does Tom Rose. Tom Rose fought in the Battle of Britain, and he has a medal to prove he was a hero but he doesn't like to talk about it and Jacob mustn't bother him or ask. Well just once, just briefly if you like, and then not again. It is very much the sort of thing, he tells the boy, a person would rather forget. Not the result of the battle, of course, but what happened to one's chums. Brave fellows, every one. Colin Baron was a gunner but Tom Rose was a pilot and you see this place where my nose bends to the side? he asks Jacob, pointing, that's where it lost an argument with the control panel when I blacked out but, thank heaven for my navigator, we made it safely home.

Henry Meyer was a partner too but he died of cancer last winter and we owe him everything, their father says, because he could see what was coming before the rest of us saw. I shall honor his memory, always, and how he bore up bravely, so very bravely at the end. He says this standing, with a drink, at the dinner they give in his honor and when he is called upon to make a toast. He says because of Henry Meyer I arrived in London, and then I met the lady who was soon to be my wife. Met her again, I mean, because of course we had first met in Germany, but here in London it was different and I well remember, Daddy says, on the day we were planning to marry, Neville Chamberlain returned from Munich and made an announcement on the wireless that there would be peace in our time. He was completely wrong, of course, but I rang up my bride-to-be and said well possibly there won't be war, do you want to call it off? And she said no, we might as well go through with it, let's just go ahead.

He lifts his glass once more. To that decision I drink; to the memory of our dear Henry Meyer and to my friends and partners and to my wife and sons. I am, he says, a fortunate man and I am very grateful, let us drink to absent friends. Johnny Weiser says *hear hear* and Gabriele Meyer is crying and the waiters bring the meat course and they all sit down again.

"Is that really true?" Tom Rose inquires, and Mummy asks him, "What?"

"That he rang you up and said, 'Well, do you want to call it off?'"

She nods. She pats her lips.

"What an extraordinary thing to do; why would he do that?"

"It's obvious, isn't it obvious?"

"No." He shakes his head. "Not to me."

"Because in peacetime we might have gone back. But don't you believe it, I never believed it, there was no possibility that we would live in Germany. That we could start our lives again as we had done before."

"But?"

"But he wanted to give me the choice. The chance. He is a dreamer, my husband, and so I said no thanks."

"Extraordinary," Tom Rose says, and then it is his turn to make a toast. Good luck, he says, the very best good luck to you at this stage of the journey, at the finish of one chapter and commencement of the next. Hear hear, says Johnny Weiser, ring out the old ring in the new, and Mummy bends her head and says he's had too much to drink, *nicht wahr,* and if he continues in this fashion he must be carried home.

V

Julia: 1964

SHE HAS ALWAYS KNOWN HERSELF to be intelligent, always been proud of intelligence, always relied on the power of thought to serve her at will and at need. She had known before the others knew that Hitler was insatiable, that such an appetite for power would continue to grow with the feeding and such thirst could not be slaked. She could tell Henry Meyer was going to die, could see it in the way he sat so carefully upright and rubbing his spine. She understood that Paul would marry by the way he put his arm protectively around the girl he brought to supper in Holne Chase that time, the tune his fingers played as though of their own volition upon her collarbone. And in each of her three pregnancies she had known she would have sons.

Then, when her boys did homework, Julia liked to sit with them and solve their problems turn by turn, helping them with French and Latin and geography and history and math. *Il naquit*, said Benjamin, when he was learning how to conjugate, and she told him that no self-respecting French person would ever use that form of *naître*, that it was absurd and the proper form of utterance would be *il est né*. But anyhow, said Benjamin, we have to learn how to use it, it's called the historical past. There is perfect and imperfect and also the pluperfect and the *passée simple* and the historical past. All right, she said, but tell your teacher that your mother thinks this is excessive and will serve no useful purpose when you speak.

Intelligence is not the point, however; it is no use to her now. She has butted up against the question of what to do, and where, and why, and the problem defeats her entirely; she might as well be a mouse on a treadmill or rat in a maze for all her intelligence helps. She has brought her children to this house, has cordoned off her family and kept them safe and clean and warm, yet cannot imagine what next thing to do with her brain. It has been wholly focused, wholly fixed upon her boys. The reason for marriage is children, Julia thinks; the reason for a home like this is how it may serve as safe haven, but her parents are dead and her eldest child Jacob is busy becoming a doctor and Benjamin has gone off to work in the gallery in London. In the watches of the night, with her husband beside her snoring, unruffled, she cannot decide what to do.

"You could help me," Karl suggests.

"How?"

"The office could use you."

"In what way?"

"I'm not, as you know, an organized person. I could use

help with the invoices, the system of the files. In the sense that we need to be organized better."

"To say the least," she says.

This does not deter him, naturally; he too can be stubborn and hear what he chooses to hear. And so he repeats his suggestion, saying they could drive together to the city twice a week, or three times, more often if she wishes, and keep each other company and she can be the set of eyes and the efficiency expert he so sorely misses in the office. Considering his offer, she knows she must refuse. Jacob is a realist and Ben a romantic and neither of her grown-up sons requires her services now; the dog requires her, of course, and their third child is still at home, *Gott sei dank*. But William—their American afterthought—will leave her also soon enough, and the house will be utterly empty. Until then, Julia tells herself, she must stay home to ask about his school day and to offer him his chocolate brownies and his glass of milk; she has done this for the others and she will not shirk such duty now, not make the last feel least.

"Well, when you're ready," Karl says.

"All right. But *filing*?"

"Not simply filing," he says.

"I'll tell you, I promise."

"Please do."

"Tu l'as voulu, Georges Dandin."

All the same he has a point; she needs to find some sort of work. She can order groceries and tell the maid to wash and wax the pantry floor and demonstrate to the laundress how best to iron the shirts, but none of this amounts to proper occupation. There are only so many hours in the day to devote to her roses and orchids; there are only so many cigarettes to smoke and *Baumkuchen* and brownies and cheese biscuits it's possible to bake. She could have been a translator but nobody asks her to translate; she could have been an interpreter and would be happy, for example, to interpret for Ralph Bunche. This is a man she respects, this is an honorable enterprise, except she knows nobody at the U.N. and in any case they would not invite a middle-aged Westchester housewife to translate ten hours a week. She has volunteered at Billy's school, but what they want her for is to shelve books or to take attendance at the reception desk. After two weeks, when she tried this, Julia could not continue, because for someone who once studied with Ernst Cassirer and would have been a doctor of philosophy if Hitler had not closed the schools or forbade Jews to be graduated, this is unworthy, an insult, not deliberate perhaps but insulting nevertheless.

Still, she would like to serve. It would help to have somewhere to go. Sometimes at the Lord & Taylor in Wykagyl or in Saks Fifth Avenue she watches the women who work behind counters—those who sell perfumes or handbags or scarves—and wonders, since they smile and smile, if she could bring herself to do such work and might find pleasure there. It isn't a question of money, of course, of needing to be paid for it but needing to be of some use. There would be a certain satisfaction in arranging the perfume and scarves. She can imagine Gucci handbags or Ferragamo shoes, for example, piled in a pyramid on counters so as to catch the eye enticingly and make a customer pause. She herself has often paused to admire such arrangements, and the abundant merchandise in Lord &

Taylor is a comfort to behold. But to become a shop girl now would be impossible, unthinkable, and she turns away. Where has it gone, her lightsome youth, her proud and glad insouciance, and how has she come to this pass?

———◦

Years ago she had had a flirtation with a friend of her brother's named Jacob Steiner who lived on the Branitzerplatz. Like all her other classmates, she fell in love on a regular basis—deciding one week in favor of Lutz, the next in favor of Udo, and this for no greater reason than the way that Lutz or Udo rolled their pants legs or their cigarettes. Julia had been flirtatious, since that had been the way of young people in Berlin, and it was fashionable to declare yourself dying of passion for a boy at a dance or costume ball and then, the next day, saying *who?* That oaf, that ox, you can't possibly mean Udo or that awful Lutz.

This had been both pleasant and amusing: a stranger or soldier or a second cousin twice removed would tip his hat to you along the avenue and you yourself would nod or fail to nod and later tell your classmates of the great adventure that befell you in the street. Outside the cinema your father's driver would be waiting in his uniform, and how he chaffed a passing housemaid would be something you observed: the way they leaned together, nearly touching, the mirroring sheen of his boots. You saw the housemaid drop her handkerchief and saw the chauffeur stop and bend to pick it up. Then of that half-heard and half-understood encounter you could construct a story and regale your girlfriends and be in turn regaled. You'll never believe what happened at the cinema, *ins Kino*, just wait till I tell you, oh Edith just wait till you hear . . .

Then it would be Edith's turn. She or Gretel or Alexandra would have also witnessed something and imagined an adventure and would describe it breathlessly, eyes wide, whispering how underneath a linden tree *this* one had gazed at her suggestively, *that* one twirled the points of his moustache, *this* one had cracked his outstretched hand so she could hear each knuckle.

Such stories were not serious, of course; they had been practice only, a prelude for the melody and performance soon to come. *Fantasiestucke*, scenes from childhood, *Kinderszenen* — so that even in the middle of her own most ardent imagined encounters she had known it was not serious. Her friends would look shocked, going pink in the cheek, and say no, not really — *really?* drawing comfort from the certainty that such and such a fantasy was not in fact the case.

But on her sixteenth birthday Julia's parents gave a party, they invited business associates and the whole neighborhood and all her friends and classmates to the house. There had been champagne and caviar and an orchestra in the rear garden, underneath the trellised roses and the climbing grapes. Her father wore his medals and her mother wore so many diamonds you fairly had to shut your eyes if she approached the chandelier; this was the period before the Reich when everything sparkled, everything shone, and her parents moved as fish through water in the element of wealth. Heinrich Tessenow arrived, with his assistant Albert Speer, and the two architects pro-

nounced themselves well, pleased with the completion of
their project. This was the time, she understands, when
her father's bank expanded and his real estate speculations
bore fruit.

Her birthday came on May 11, and she was flirtatious
and bored. She received the guests' attentions, *natürlich*,
and there were toasts and gifts, but it was fashionable to
be bored and so Julia stood on the veranda in her birthday gown and waited for someone to ask her to dance.
Her father's partners in the bank, and his clerks and office managers and white-haired upright Professor Cassirer
from across the street approached her with their compli-
ments and kindly praise until she, Julia, wanted to die.
Nothing happened; nothing would ever happen to her, ever,
and she would grow bitter and ugly and old and life would
be lonely and dull.

Her brother Fritz had lady friends; he was a dandy, a
Don Juan, and liked to go skiing in the Swiss Alps with
the fast set from the university; he showed her photographs
of girls, their hair undone, teeth brilliant, in snow-bright
meadows and on hillsides holding skis. When she said oh,
let me go with you, oh do please teach me how to ski, he
said not yet, little sister, not yet.

Then there was a *coup de foudre*; then everything, all of
it changed. She heard her brother's low-pitched laugh and
saw him approach the veranda, holding a tall stranger's
arm. His hair was brown, his nose was strong, he had the
cheekbones of a conqueror and in his patent leather pumps
stood precisely at her brother's height; shoulder to shoulder, they mounted the steps. The young men appeared on
excellent terms; they both wore evening clothes. His name

was Jacob; he studied philosophy and had rooms on the Branitzerplatz. She did not know this yet, of course, did not yet even know his name, but Fritz introduced them and said, bending, whispering into her ear. *Here, little sister, this is your present, the one of all our company who knows how to ski best of all.*

There had been blossoms everywhere, and a silver moon. Jacob asked her to dance. They danced. They did so in the garden, on the lawn. It was very many years ago, and she cannot remember a word they exchanged or the name of the tune the orchestra played or if her girlfriends and her parents too were dancing; all this has been erased. And she has come to know, *natürlich,* how foolish and romantic is virginity, how much she took for granted then that was not hers to take. But thirty-five years afterwards she still can feel the weakness in her knees, the guiding pressure of his hand in the small of her back and twirling down the paving stones and past the little fountain where the orchestra was stationed. She remembers the increasing dark, the ringing in her ears, the lanterns in the hedgerow and the way he blotted out the light because her head was nestled at his shoulder and his evening clothes were black. She remembers the smell of his eau de cologne, of brandy and old cigarettes, the sweat at the clean-shaven line of his neck and how wetly warm it felt upon her fingers when she cupped her hand there finally and, finally, they kissed.

～～

Julia sits in the library, waiting. Lighting a cigarette with her father's initialed platinum lighter, the one he had

had in his pocket, escaping, she watches the blown smoke disperse. Benjamin promised to call. Because it is too soon for gin, she has eaten a cheese biscuit and poured a glass of sherry, and the sun is bright beyond the French doors of the library and on the snow on the balcony railing. Last night it snowed, a dusting only, a few flakes, but there had been serious snow two days before and it remains too cold to melt except for the icicles under the eaves. These late spring storms are daunting; the snow is wet and heavy and comes just when you tell yourself, at last it will be spring. It is not difficult to understand the problem, but to state is not to solve it: she will go mad in the house.

Benjamin has not, she knows, enjoyed his stay in England, and this to some degree confirms how right she was in 1948 to make them emigrate. As to the matter of having left England, she had not had a moment's regret. The gallery in Cork Street is profitable, however, and a question of succession attaches to success; although none of the partners is considering retirement, it is understood between them that they require someone of the "younger generation." Miss Burleigh has no children; Henry Tolland has a son who worked in the business some years before but fought with his father and left; Gustave's daughter, Elizabeth-Anne, shows no interest in the field. And now that he has finished college Ben-Ben needs a *Wanderjahr*; he has always been artistic and perhaps this profession will suit. So we will try each other on for size, her brother-in-law informed her, we'll see how the hand fits the glove . . .

Where the icicles drip they make ice on the porch. Beyond, the pines are white. He has arranged to telephone from Cork Street, before he departs for the evening, and that will be at five o'clock with a five-hour differential, so now that it is nearly noon she can expect Ben's call. She folds the *New York Times* in half—she values James Reston and reads what he writes—and pours a second drink.

Time flies; time stops; time races or crawls while we endure it; we are creatures in its thrall. She is fifty-one years old. Because Thursday is the maid's day off, and Billy not yet back from school, she sits by herself in the house. Her cigarette is finished but she does not light another; she could listen to, but does not, WQXR. The dog is sleeping at her feet, twitching expectantly as it trees cats or brings a squirrel back to her feet in its dreams. And somehow such expectancy makes Julia feel more lonely still, more silent in the silent room where the clock ticks and the phone does not ring. What she hears is the furnace, the snuffling intake of the poodle's breath, the icicles melting outside, and none of her vaunted intelligence helps; nothing makes it better that she waits for him to call.

The telephone rings. For the sake of self-control she waits three rings before picking it up, but when she says "Hello" the voice on the line is not Ben's but Dr. Rieser's secretary calling from his office and confirming the appointment for her teeth to be cleaned tomorrow morning at eleven. "Is that still convenient?" the woman asks, and she wants to say how can we ever know what it is tomorrow brings, my dentist's appointment or general annihilation; who can tell? We act, however, as if we know, *als ob*; we live in the provisional moment and at this particular moment I intend to come to your office and have my teeth cleaned, yes.

"Fine," says the receptionist brightly. "See you tomorrow, then."

No sooner does she replace the receiver than, once more, the telephone rings. This time she does not wait to lift it from its cradle but this time it is her husband, calling from the office, telling her he's off to lunch and has a conference at two o'clock and has had difficulty with the warehouse manager again this morning because he arrived late and, Karl could swear it, drunk. He calls three times a day at least, and often four or five times to inform her of his whereabouts, and when he will be coming home—on which train if he takes the train, or when he's setting out to drive if that morning he has used the car—and although she's grateful for the human contact and the frequent bulletins she cannot bring herself, today, to prolong the discussion of where he will be eating lunch or what is wrong with warehouse personnel.

He says goodbye, and she does too, and the wind outside shifts suddenly and covers the panes with blown snow.

———

Julia understands, *natürlich*, that everyone must have a first romantic fling, and sooner or later the first fling will end. Young people die, but not for love, and this has been self-evident since Shakespeare; a single kiss in a dark garden must come to a conclusion, and the orchestra will put away its instruments and fold its chairs and the dance and the party will end. A heart does not stop; the world will not stop; things continue as before.

Except it did not end. It could not be erased. On the

surface what they did and said together was without importance; they danced one dance and kissed one kiss and
an intelligent person must understand that matters would
continue as before. She met Jacob Steiner afterwards two
or three times possibly; she saw him at a distance, often,
those first months. He was her brother's friend who paid
polite attention if she chanced to pass him in the hallway
or pretended that it was by chance they met outside in the
street. But nothing more happened between them; he was
aloof and disengaged and she had been sixteen years old.
It did not matter to him that there'd been a *coup de foudre*
and that she was his for the asking if he but deigned to
notice and then, noticing, to ask.

In September Jacob appeared at the house, telling Fritz
he was leaving for Greece. Then for a year he pursued his
education and continued with his studies of philosophy and
when *endlich* he returned—lean and dark and sporting a
moustache—he came unannounced to the door. She and
her brother had been playing chess and listening to Schubert and now once again Jacob joined them and they put
away the chessboard—*jiocco piano*, it would be a draw—
and Fritz asked him how his work had gone and how his
thesis progressed. He was considering, said Jacob, the end
of Friedrich Hölderlin's life as a productive poet and the
famous gnomic utterance, *Apollon hat mich geschlagen.* This
phrase was, he explained, at one and the same time a
learned allusion to the god Apollo and the condition of
Enlightenment and a poor madman's pronouncement—
coming off a walking tour—that he had suffered sunstroke
while wandering in the Alps. Hölderlin himself proclaimed

that he had been struck by Apollo, and then the poet went insane and never wrote again.

This represents, said Jacob, as far as I'm concerned, the essential duality in the soul of Germany, the paradox and conflict at the heart of our own culture; it is not so much a play on words as *Schauspiel* and proof of Platonic duality; both of these readings are true. Is it not the case—he laughed—we take our Apollo *mit Schlag*. He and Fritz continued in this manner, speaking of Winckelmann and Goethe and Jacob's thesis that the German soul was a divided one, and while he and Fritz were discussing the Enlightenment and madness she, Julia, thought she would also go mad; she wanted only to kiss him again, only to feel his new bristling moustache and dance in the dark in his arms.

Jacob spoke about the Parthenon and the antiquities of Athens and the beauty of the temple which he visited at Delphi and the fabled wine-dark or, more properly, wine-*light* Aegean sea. He lit a cigarette. By now she had been seventeen, a full-grown woman, or nearly, but he failed to notice; crossing his legs and rocking back and forth abstractedly, exhaling rings of smoke, he continued to speak to her brother, and when she arrived at his rooms the next day, on the pretext that he'd left his copy of *Laocöon* at their house, with his own notes on the pages and would surely want the volume returned, and therefore she had come to see him on the way back to her house from school, and since his door had been unlocked she climbed the stairs and knocked and entered, taking the liberty, trusting he'd not object, Jacob did not even bother to stand and make her welcome or hang up her coat.

The door, he said, it was unlocked? and she said yes and he said in that case lock it, why not.

He was in his shirtsleeves and lying in a haze of smoke, a bottle of champagne half-finished on the floor. They finished the champagne. She asked, do you have more, don't you have anything else for a girl? and he produced another bottle and they continued to drink. Wildly daring, Julia swallowed glass after glass, until finally her thirst was slaked and he said, *Sagen sie mir,* why have you come here in this fashion, what is it you expect? Not blushing, kicking off her shoes, she said *Herr* Steiner, I expect you will now make a woman of me, please. She hung her dress over the chair. It was Berlin and 1930 and this was how people behaved. She can remember with no difficulty everything that happened next, as well as what failed to happen: the way she took off the rest of her clothes while he looked at her unblinkingly, then turned his back upon her and faced the painted wall. She stood beside him disregarded, burning not so much with shame as with schoolgirl confusion: *what do we do now?*

Then after some moments he rose from the bed—gracefully, carefully smiling—and draped his coat across her naked shoulders and said *Schön,* we must understand each other, I must explain to you some things about the world. Your brother is my friend but you are not my *Freundin,* and I am gentleman enough to leave you quite alone. I am gentleman enough, he said, to make manifest the difference between illusion and delusion, and what you want to give today is not for me to take—impossible, unsuitable. I must complete my studies first and then perhaps we may resume a courtship; your father is a wealthy man, someone with proper expectations for his daughter's marriage, and what we do together must be done in daylight, properly. We cannot be careless, my dear.

He continued to smile but not with mirth, with what she now believes was pain, a stricken foreknowledge of failure and loss, and poured champagne until it overflowed her glass and he filled and tamped his pipe and, inhaling deeply, said to her as darkness fell and outside they were lighting lamps, well, little girl, have you been enlightened here, were you invaded by Apollo, yes or no?

What happened to her in that room was neither simple nor rapid; what happened afterwards was history and Hitler and her shocked horror and recrimination and regrets. Years later, when he killed himself, when it was clear that Hitler would intern and starve and destroy him unless he, Jacob Steiner, anticipated and forestalled this and fell not so much upon his sword as from the fourth-story window of his room on the Branitzerplatz—wearing his dress clothes, a white silk scarf around his neck, a white rose pinned above the yellow star—Julia came to understand that this was her secret to keep.

She did not tell Edith or Gretel or anyone else what it felt like, up there on the chair, not in some imagined passionate embrace but trying not to cry and staring at the painting in the gilt frame on the wall. It had been a landscape, that much she can remember, and there had been a waterfall and sheep.

Nor could she tell her brother in the years to come. When Fritz said happy birthday and left her in the arms of a dance partner and they found the darkness at the garden's end, her brother understood, or seemed to, that everything would change. But that had been the limit of his interest—a ski trip and flirtation was the limit of what her brother imagined—and she did not betray her knowledge to him either; it was not his concern.

Her brother had been fortune's child; he was handsome and well favored and, until the time of the Nazis, carefree; when their parents sailed for Cuba, Fritz walked across the Pyrenees to make his own escape. He had gone mountain climbing and sailing and played tennis with the children of the rich; he reported on his escapades—how he wore the costume of Mozart's Cherubino in a masked ball, for instance, and how he went home afterwards with a woman who dressed as the Duchess and serenaded her *falsetto*, until she said to him, laughing, good sir your voice will crack. Come with me now upstairs . . .

There would be other men, of course: eligible suitors and ineligible suitors, a lawyer from Bremen, Paul's father, an assistant to the rector of the university where she, in turn, studied Winckelmann and Schopenhauer and read the verse of Hölderlin—there would be many others in the passing of her innocence, but none surpassing the first. When Jacob fastened the rose to his jacket and leapt with what she knew would be his bitter feigned insouciance from the window to the pavement, he took along her *Kinderszenen* and the *Fantasiestucke* also; the scenes from her protected childhood and her maiden fantasies were crushed as absolutely as had been his skull. And when at last she married Karl and settled down and settled in, she gave her first son Jacob's name so as not to forget, to never forget and always be reminded of that first romantic adventure, her daring intransigent wide-eyed youth and intelligent stupidity that day.

~~~

She lights a cigarette. She puts on reading glasses and tries to pay attention to the *New York Times*. Bosley Crowther has an article about the Italian directors he so much admires — Fellini, Da Sica, Antonioni — and how the locus of artistic energy has shifted away from Hollywood today in the making of films. Tomorrow he will write about Jean Renoir, François Truffaut, Jean-Luc Godard and the French. Julia peruses with some interest the details of his argument, the things the critic writes about the studio system and creative independence, the examples he provides of European excellence. When the telephone rings a third time it is what she hoped for, as in the old stories, her son.

His voice is surprisingly clear. "Hi, Mom," he says. "How are you?"

"Fine."

"How's everything going?" he asks.

She tells him fine, repeating this, and he asks about the weather and she tells him that it snowed; then she asks about the weather in London, and he says it rarely snows but there's a cold rain often, does she remember the sleet and the darkness, and she tells him yes. He asks about his father and his brothers and she asks about his uncle and his grandmother and aunt. In the midst of this inconsequence she eats another biscuit and he asks what am I hearing? and she says a poor connection, and he says I went to Kent last month, a place called Sandhurst-

Hawkhurst, it's very pretty there and it looked almost like spring. Please give our best regards to Steffi, Julia says, I sent flowers when we heard about her mother but of course I haven't heard if the bouquet arrived. She died peacefully, says Ben, Mrs. Feingold collapsed drinking soup. After a moment Julia asks how does it go in Lyndhurst Road—have they put in central heating yet?—and Ben says no, not really, it's still just the paraffin stoves.

I cannot understand, she says, how they can live so shabbily and be so very rich.

They don't seem to notice, he says, or if they do notice, don't care.

It's a matter of comfort, she tells him, and keeping up appearances; they should not be so shabby and should have adequate heat. In a living room with an important Peter Paul Rubens on the wall, it's a form of ostentation to use only paraffin stoves.

The poodle stretches, sleeping. When he wakes there'll be a biscuit; if the snow truly stops they might walk. In the crystal ashtray at her side Julia stubs out the cigarette and takes another from the case but does not light it yet. How has Benjamin managed without her; how will she prevent whatever harm awaits from troubling or afflicting him; how might she at this distance intervene? She asks if he remembers what it felt like years ago to go to that musical on Broadway, *La Plume de Ma Tante,* and when he asks her why she says that William's French class is learning exactly that sequence: *J'entre dans la salle de classe. Je regarde autour de moi,* she says, that's what he's learning to do. When I regard what's around me I see only the dog and the snow, she declares, and Benjamin asks her, Mom, is everything really all right?

Of course it is, she says.

He says he misses her; she says she misses him.

Is there anything you need? she asks, and he tells her thank you, no.

We've been discussing a visit, she says, your father must make a business trip and perhaps you'd like to meet in Italy or Greece?

I'm writing stories, he tells her, I'm trying to learn how to write.

They can't take what you carry in your head, she says, as she has said to him often. He agrees. Some somewhere warm, says Julia, and recites the line from Baudelaire: *"'N'importe où, hors de ce monde.'"* Anywhere out of this world.

"It hasn't worked," he tells her.

The dog growls, still asleep. She empties her glass. "What?"

"The gallery. I can't talk about it now."

"Is Gustave there?"

"No."

"Tolland? Lillian?" Perhaps—she regards the animal doubtfully—a walk will help.

"No, nobody," he says. "But I don't feel like discussing it from the office telephone. If you know what I mean."

"I don't," she says. "I don't know what you mean. I don't have the slightest idea."

"The foggiest," he says.

"Excuse me?"

"The foggiest notion," he says. "That's the expression they use over here."

"I remember. What will come to pass will come to pass."

"Yes."

"Try not to forget it, will you? The dead and the forgotten are together in my custody."

"Excuse me?"

"It's an expression," she says.

And then they say goodbye.

———～———

It is 12:17. We are time's playthings, she tells herself, drinking dry sherry and eating a cheese biscuit, its keepers and calendar markers. We are the fools of time. Julia has a vision, swallowing, of a day a decade later when her children and grandchildren will gather to hear Schubert, "Death and the Maiden," the slow movement, in the recording by the Budapest Quartet, or perhaps the Amadeus—this precise she cannot be, or does not choose to be, no longer caring to make such distinctions. Her sons will be well dressed and austere in their demeanor and their manners will be excellent; they will greet those who join them to mourn. There will be a procession of cars. There will be many whose lives she has touched—the laundress and librarian and the owners of the single good bookstore in town and the couple who ran Broderson's and those who work for her husband and those with whom she played canasta or chess. This will transpire at the cemetery where both her parents lie. Paul will have come, of course, driving down from Ithaca, and Nora Meyer Unterwald will arrive by airplane, and her brother, her dear brother and his family. There will be flowers, the orchids she raises and tends with such skill, and no doubt carnations and roses and perhaps a Bird of Paradise in an arrangement with lilies, but lilies are vulgar and predictable and she hopes there are no flowers specific to a funeral at this particular funeral; it is better, always, to go against the grain and to expect the unexpected in death as well as life.

Her three sons will have married; the eldest and the youngest will marry childhood sweethearts, and they will do so while young. But Benjamin will wander and take his own time, choosing, and bring back a succession of women to her house. For years she will endure the presence of his girlfriends and then, when he grows older, lady friends; she will force herself to make them welcome, turn by turn. There will be blondes and redheads and brunettes; there will be short and tall ones, Jew and Gentile, large and small. Then finally her second son will settle down, proposing to a girl she has already met in passing, the daughter of a cellist, and they will have two daughters of their own.

His wife, Elena, will be pregnant by the time of the funeral service and Jacob's wife will have produced three children, and William, her youngest, will also have wed and soon enough his bride too will conceive and so there will be several generations attending this occasion in the room.

But what of the elders, her elders? Of these there will be few. The Nazis saw to that. Adela and Albert and Edith and Peter and Hans and Lilo and Felicia will huddle together, muttering, as though of all the insults that the flesh

189

must suffer the final insult is that they outlive her who was, by comparison, young. The best thing of all is not to be born, according to the ancients, and the next best thing is to die young—but with this she disagrees. She would have welcomed longer life. She would prefer to live. Her husband, Karl—angelic man, she knows that now—will sit with the expression on his face she saw when his own mother died, and when Henry Meyer died, the stunned expression of an ox whose skull has been crushed as a kindness preparatory to slaughter and who understands but managed to forget that the way of the world is woe, woe.

All this she sees on the instant, emptying her glass. She lights a cigarette. Sun melts the snow beyond. In the pattern of its melting it is not like rain precisely, not a series of raindrops that course down the pane but rather as though it were crystalline breath, the breath for a chill instant coalescing, all-pervasive, and then evanescent, exhaled. The filigree of snow becomes, once more, bright air. It falls in a clump from the eaves. She herself will die of a brain tumor; she will be sixty-one.

Her illness will be brief. On the day before Thanksgiving Julia will drop a knife and, reaching for it, not be able to retrieve or feel the blade or control her fingers when she straightens up, and the doctors will suggest she might perhaps have suffered a small stroke but they will not be hopeful and their faces will be grave and her eldest son Jacob, the doctor, will after consultation prepare the family for the worst and soon enough the tests will prove that what is wrong is inoperable, a cancer lodged and growing in her brain. It will not be benign. In her brain the edema will swell and enlarge till all she wants and needs and can accomplish is sleep. If there be such a thing as mercy the location of the tumor will prove merciful. From the day of diagnosis it will take only three months; she will die in her own bed upstairs.

Her husband will be sketching, trying to preserve her face and sitting at her side. He will look up from his sketch-pad, eyes narrowed and lips pursed, saying, "Just a minute, *Augenblick*," and will confirm that she is not asleep or breathing before he calls the nurse. Then because Karl will yield to her wishes she will be cremated, not buried, be-cause she loves the earth more than the faith her ances-tors professed which says she should be buried as a body in the earth.

And when she will be granule and bone the urn con-taining all she is will go with Benjamin, the one she held in her embrace while he was at death's door when ten, the one she feared that she might lose and carried to the bath-room, the apple of her eye, her second son who—having discussed it with his father and his brothers—will hire a small propeller plane in the mountains she so much en-joys, the Green Mountains of Vermont where he has gone to live and work, and where she has visited often, and ad-mired the view, and with two friends in suits and ties, wearing a top hat and carrying champagne, fly out of the Bennington Airport and over farms and villages and cross-roads he identifies until the winding river valley, with its wisps of cloud and sawmills and pine stands and lakes and barns, becomes an unknown landscape and place he can-not recognize, the intersection of hilltops and cliff, a ridge of old growth somewhere north, and leaning forward will call, "Here?" and the pilot will climb and then bank and agree to it, "Here!"; Ben will open the window, securing the flap, surprised by the roar of the engines and the strength of their created wind, and force the urn out at the end of his arm and uncap and tip it, pouring, streaming ash until what remains is dispersed.

Epilogue

London, 1996

I WALK GUSTAVE to the tube. We have rented a flat for the summer, but our visit to London is ending and he came to say goodbye. He has arrived for breakfast and we cover the table with food: pastries, toast, juice, jam, eggs, bacon, coffee, tea. "I have no appetite," he says, and proceeds to slather butter on his bread. "I can taste nothing, nothing," and stirs three spoons of sugar in his tea.

Our daughters look away. They have been trying not to laugh; they marvel at the marmalade he layers so thickly on cake. "It's pointless to cook for me, pointless," Gustave repeats to Elena. "I lost my taste buds long ago and notice nothing at all. But I will take one slice of toast in order to be sociable if it makes you happy, my dear . . ."

The flat is owned by a society painter who decamps for the summer to Devon; he flees, he has told me confidingly, the tourists and the heat. We have been happy here. The place is high-ceilinged and quirkily furnished—a grand piano in the bedroom, a dining table for twelve in the foyer, a bell jar with twenty-eight hummingbirds perched on a tin tree. Porcelain dogs flank the fireplace grate; a large gilt-framed mirror in the entrance hall doubles the prospect for those who arrive. The kitchen gives out on a garden and the bathroom is painted ripe plum.

Our daughters—Francesca, twenty-two, and Andrea, eighteen—have been visiting and, since London in the summer is a place young people gather, so have several of their friends. Bought in the time when such purchase was cheap, the flat is what estate agents describe as *commodious* and the furnishings *artistic*: flocked wallpaper and threadbare Orientals and draped easels in the library behind a trundle bed. There's a mural in the corridor painted by our landlord, with representations of himself as a satyr, a British sailor, and even as a cherub flying over what looks like the Rock of Gibraltar and strumming a guitar.

Gustave is ninety-two. His cheeks are pink—he powders them—his shock of hair bright white. He is wearing his blue suit, his blue-and-yellow-striped tie. Some time ago he relinquished his pipe; when he no longer could taste the tobacco it seemed wasteful, he tells me, to smoke. In the years since Steffi died he has seen little of their daughter; they do not get along. "We have nothing to say to each other," he says. *"Leider, wir verstehen uns nicht."*

All summer I have told myself this might be our final visit and the last season we meet. Although the house on Lyndhurst Road has its complement of boarders, he spends his days alone. "Madame La Fata has been kind," he says, but when I watch him in repose his face is grim. Brine gathers in the corners of his eyes. Nevertheless he retains his opinions: the artistic impulse has been impoverished in this atomic age, he reminds me, and people are parochial, particularly Americans, and twelve percent of the nation is left-handed whereas only three percent are ambidextrous and he plans to brush up on his Russian in order to read *War and Peace* in the great original and although the doctors warned him that he should avoid too much butter and sugar he has never had the slightest difficulty with diabetes. Yet each of the doctors who warned him—Samson and Lucas and those who came after—is dead.

Pevsner has died, and Gombrich; Kenneth Clark has died and, long before him, Berenson; in America Meyer Shapiro has died. The art historians are gone, and so are the artists themselves. They are all dead, his glad companions, J. B. Priestley and Elias Canetti and Henry Moore and Max Beckmann: those who fled from Hitler or came into the gallery or made him welcome in their studios or lived nearby. In the long sonata of the dead—the learned and the winsome and the cultured and vivacious—there is now only this diminishing reprise. His sight is bad. His eyes which have served him so well for so long are failing, as his mother's did, and he goes everywhere with a magnifying glass on a chain around his neck. He keeps one in his pocket also, just in case. When he walks into a room, our room, it is a dark blur.

"Atrocious," he says of the mural. Above the mantel hangs a pastel portrait of a youthful Princess Diana, done by our landlord from life. "A French bordel," he says, and points to an oil painting of a statue in a garden, its marble colored like flesh. "And typically English in its tastelessness, such *kitsch.*"

Yet if he has no use for what is hanging on the walls, he takes great pleasure in the company of these three "delightful ladies," as he calls them, and as "a student of physiognomy" approves of our daughters, my beautiful wife. They smile and offer him another piece of bacon and another slice of cake. He peers at them attentively, assessing this one's profile, that one's shape. "Tell me," he inquires, "which one of you is literary and which one likes to dance?"

❧

It is 1996, mid-August, and today is our last day. By noon he is ready to leave. I conduct him to the door and help him into his raincoat—first the left sleeve, then the right. He embraces our daughters lingeringly, and I wonder if he also feels we might not meet again. "How fortunate I am," he says, "that we should share a last name. Charming, charming." They stand on the landing and wave.

Where we live is just three streets away from the Wetherby Gardens I stayed in that chill winter while working in his gallery more than half my life before. All summer I have wandered, assessing what is constant and what changed. The area has grown respectable and the value of real estate increased exponentially, so that my rooming house with its cats on the stairwell and rubbish bins behind the gate is now a millionaire's address. Its facade has been repointed and its stucco gleams.

But Earl's Court itself resists gentrification; the streets still teem with students, and there's a seedy international swarming, always, at the entrance to the tube. Much bustle on the pavement: backpackers and postmen, bank messengers and pickpockets, the fumes of motorbikes and marijuana, the singsong call of vendors—newspaper sellers, tobacconists—the purposive striding of those in a hurry, the loitering saunter of those who are not. For weeks the London underground service has been disrupted and subject to strikes, and it's never clear how often or how rapidly the trains will run. I've urged Gustave to order a car. Or I could hail a taxi and arrange him on the seat and tell the driver where to go. He says, "Nonsense, not a bit of it, I'll take the train. The walk from Belsize Park will do me good."

So we proceed to Earl's Court. The day is hot and dry. Gustave carries an umbrella as a walking stick, and he pauses every fifty feet, examining the windows and the flowerpots in doorways and children with their dogs. "*Ach ja,*" he says repeatedly, his intonation just like his mother's, and I wonder if I too will use that phrase in years to come. I want to say something important, to tell him that he represents, for me, a lasting link in childhood's chain and that I understand his dogma and abstraction and his brusque acerbity are hedged against catastrophe, and that I love him for it except we do not say such things and so I ask instead if he will visit America for the auctions in the autumn, and he tells me no. I tell him I'll return to London as soon as possible, perhaps next spring, and he says, "Yes. Do try."

At the entrance to the tube a tall black woman wearing four-inch heels walks back and forth seductively, and it takes till the third pass before I see she is a man. The flower stall is open, rank on rank of bright profusion, and the vendor is drinking hot tea. Gustave extracts his wallet and, after protracted fumbling, offers me a ten-pound note. "Buy Elena some flowers," he says. I thank him for his generosity and say it is not necessary; we are leaving in the morning and the flowers will be wasted. "Buy them anyhow," he says. *"Auf Wiedersehen,* my dear."

Then he takes out his tube pass and waves it at the inspector and advances through the barricade and although I could follow I do not but stand instead watching this beak-nosed small bent ancient man with the white thatch of hair and umbrella and blue raincoat in the crowd of those who hover at the elevator's door. He does not turn around. Next winter he will die. At length the elevator arrives, disgorging its cargo of passengers, a throng that disperses while those who are waiting advance. My uncle stands irresolute until the elevator man says, "Sir?" and moves aside to urge him in and finally now lost to view he steps behind the sliding, closing doors.